A Wisconsin Dells thriller!

Return
of
Elijah

T0204804

by Father Dale Grubba

Waubesa Press
The quality fiction imprint
of Badger Books, Inc.

© Copyright 2001 by Dale Grubba
Published by Waubesa Press,
the quality fiction imprint of Badger Books Inc.

Printed by McNaughton & Gunn of Saline, Mich.

First Edition

ISBN 1-878569-75-9

Badger Books Inc.
P.O. Box 192
Oregon, WI 53575
Toll-free phone: (800) 928-2372
Web site: http://www.badgerbooks.com
E-mail: books@badgerbooks.com

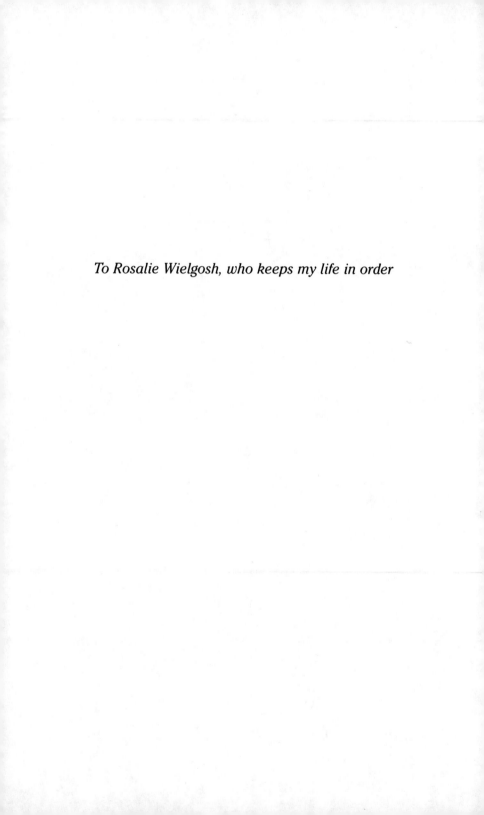

To Rosalie Wielgosh, who keeps my life in order

Introduction

Too often in literature, and indeed society, people with mental illness are portrayed as monsters. In fact, they are sons, daughters, mothers and fathers with families who love them deeply. Father Grubba knows this. His book paints the true picture of the agony a family endures when one of their own is crippled by madness.

The National Institute of Mental Health estimates that as many as one in four of all people will suffer from, mental illness at one point or another in their lives. That's staggering. Consider that for every person with mental illness, another four or five are directly impacted by them. It's not too much of a stretch, then, to say that nearly everyone's life is touched by mental illness.

Most mentally ill people are not violent and do not act out their fantasies. However, it does happen, and the consequences can be devestating. You can pick up any newspaper any day of the week and find some family whose lives have been turned upside down by mental illness.

The law does not do enough to protect these people from themselves. The emphasis is on protecting the patient's privacy and his or her civil liberties. These are noble goals, but not at the expense of getting those with illnesses the help they need to live well.

It's messy. As this book shows, there are no easy answers and, sometimes, things go terribly wrong.

— **Meg Kissinger**
Milwaukee Journal Sentinel

1

"**B**less me, Father, for I have sinned. It has been five years since my last confession. I accuse myself of the following sins."

A pause. The voice on the other side of the confessional screen continued, "I'm confused. Sometimes I think it was murder. I hear the voice of Satan...but I know it was the work of God."

It was a quiet Saturday in early May. Visitors filled the river town of Wisconsin Dells, Wisconsin. Its winter population of 2,500 had swelled to daily numbers of 90,000. Attractions, such as Noah's Ark Amusement Park, recorded as many as 16,000 people going through its gates in a single day. Still, the number of confessions at St. Bridget's was minimal. The people of the parish were too busy taking advantage of the short three-month tourist season to take a Saturday afternoon off, and the tourists were too busy having fun to think of repentance.

Even if everyone in Wisconsin Dells had not been busy, there would have been few confessions. The Catholic Church had lost its long line of penitents waiting along the wall for their turn in the confessional. Now priests took books along to pass the time while waiting for the occasional sinner.

Such was the case with Fr. Michael Ross, the 55-year-old pastor of St. Bridget's. Expecting no one, he was prepared to go over his sermon one more time as he sat in the confessional during the 4:30 to 5 p.m. shift.

A half-hour earlier, Fr. Ross had stopped briefly to enjoy the cool shade of the trees as he made the short walk from the rectory to the sacristy entrance. He climbed the black metal steps to the door, flipped on the lights and looked out into the main body of the church. No one was waiting so he took a few moments to move the ribbons in the books on the altar and pulpit to the proper pages for the 5:30 Mass. He filled the ciboriums with hosts and carried them, along with the wine and water, to a table in the back of church. They would be carried up during the offertory procession at Mass.

At St. Bridget's the confessional was in the back of church. While a lot of churches had made the post Vatican II changes and built a confessional room with its screen, table, chairs, and comfortable atmosphere, St. Bridget's still had the standard blond oak confessional. The priest sat in a center compartment and listened to the confessions of those who entered the compartments on either side of him. There wasn't a room on the church's main floor that could be converted to a confessional room, and Fr. Ross felt his older penitents would have difficulty getting up and down the stairs leading to the basement, so why make the change and drive away the few confessions he still heard?

He opened the confessional door and flipped the switches that activated the lights and a small overhead fan. When pressure was applied to a switch under the kneeler on the penitent's side, a red light would automatically go on over the outside of the door to indicate that the compartment was occupied. The fan carried away the heat and stale air of the priest's compartment.

There was still no one in church as Fr. Ross sat down on the swivel chair, placed the violet stole that was a symbol of repentance over his shoulders, and pulled the confessional door shut.

He was finishing the first review of his notes when he heard the door next to him open. As the penitent knelt, Fr. Ross turned slightly in the chair and slid open the small wooden door that separates sinner and priest at face level.

The opening had been routine. Five years since his

last confession, while it would have been considered a
long time years ago, was easy to conceive in the modern church. It was the sin that challenged Fr. Ross'
twenty-six years of hearing confessions. In all those
years, murder had never been the subject. Fr. Ross
heard himself asking: "Murder?"

"I'm confused," the voice responded.

"What is it that confuses you?"

"The shadow in the newspaper," said the voice with
more intensity. "Lucifer. Others couldn't see him, but I
could. He moved among the buildings in the picture.
His voice told me to kill. And when I did kill that person's
dying words were, 'I hope you rot in hell!' It was the
Prince of Devils who tricked me. Now I'm condemned
to hell!...To rot in hell!"

"When did this occur?" Fr. Ross asked, hoping to get
a few details upon which to make a judgment about
whether it was fact or fiction. He was searching for a
thread of sanity, thinking of another young man, a parishioner who had burned out on drugs.

"In the land of Genesis," replied the voice, obviously
irritated. "When giants walked this earth and man's
every thought and inclination was evil. The earth was
corrupt in the sight of God! Cain raised his knife against
Abel, and Abel's blood soaked the ground beneath him."

Whatever he was dealing with, Fr. Ross knew that it
was a problem far greater than any five minutes in a
confessional could heal. "Would it be possible for you
to come to the rectory?" he asked. "This seems like a
much larger problem than we can deal with in these
few minutes. Would you come to see me or go to see
another priest?"

Not a sound came from the other side of the screen.
Fr. Ross waited. The silence seemed forever. Then Fr.
Ross broke it, "If you really did commit a murder you
should talk to someone about it. You would feel better
if you did. God would forgive you..."

"God doesn't have to forgive me. I am God's messenger." The voice, confused and irritated before, burst forth in confidence. The person seemed to have forgotten he was in a confessional.

Fr. Ross wondered if anyone else was in the church. He tried to calm the man.

"God raised me up to destroy the evil inclinations of man," the voice said even louder, its tone hardened to a quality that frightened Fr. Ross.

"I am the faithful one in a land of sin." The curtain between them moved with the force of the breath propelling the words at Fr. Ross. "I am a son of God. A faithful one. Like Abraham, I have raised my hand over the altar and killed the evil one. The flames of Elijah have leapt up to consume him. He will rot in hell, not me! I will kill all the wicked priests of Baal."

Fr. Ross heard the door of the confessional slam open. Heavy, strident steps disappeared out of the entrance of the church. Suddenly it was quiet. If there was another person waiting, he or she did not come forth. Fr. Ross wished there had been someone. Even though they, like he, were bound never to reveal anything overheard while waiting to go to confession, Fr. Ross would have felt a lot more comfortable knowing he shared the rantings of the mysterious person whose loud voice had filled not only the confessional but all of St. Bridget's.

The voice had upset him. Priests were trained to forget the contents of confessions as soon as they had finished hearing them. In the days before Saturday Masses, confessions in larger parishes with more than one priest were often followed with cocktails, dinner and light conversation as a means of helping one forget what had gone before. Even if such had been the case, Fr. Ross knew he would not forget this confession or voice.

He tried to calm himself by thinking of the town of Wisconsin Dells and the people it attracted during the summer. He remembered his first summer, now fifteen years ago, when he had mentioned before the dismissal at a ten o'clock Mass, that Bibles were being sold after

Mass in an effort to raise funds for repairs in the cemetery. Suddenly a man had stood up in the middle of the congregation and yelled, "To hell with the Bibles, on with the Mass." An embarrassed companion, presumably his wife, had dragged him to his knees, but not before he had brought a stilled hush among the worshippers. A tourist, no doubt, who somehow evaded Fr. Ross after Mass and disappeared but left a story to be told and retold by those who had witnessed it.

Then he remembered the Sunday he had finished Mass and was standing outside the church greeting the worshippers as they left. A middle-aged woman, with two children and a husband in tow, approached him to tell about her miracle.

"The Blessed Mother appeared in our front yard," she said as the husband, who was following in her wake, rolled his eyes in anticipation of a story he was only too familiar with and wished he could interrupt.

"It was evening," said the woman, a scarf over her head in honor of the old but discontinued rule that women must wear hats in church. "She appeared on the bird bath as I was watering the lawn. She told me to leave our present home and travel to a place with tall pointed trees. I've been looking at the pine trees in this area and I think she may have meant this city."

Fr. Ross sincerely hoped not, politely reminding her that she was on the edge of an area in Wisconsin where pine trees were common. The farther north she traveled, the more evident it would become. He never saw the lady or her beleaguered family again and trusted that she had forgotten the revelation or found some other destination as its fulfillment.

Perhaps Fr. Ross' Saturday afternoon visitor could be dismissed as another in the long list of characters who had presented themselves at the doors of St. Bridget's and then were never heard from again. Those were his thoughts as the half-hour came to a close and he prepared to step from the confessional and finish preparing for the 5:30 Mass. Soon people would begin to arrive.

After flipping off the switches on the confessional, he made his way through the wide double doors in the back of the church to a closet in the vestibule and took out a broom handle that had been sawed off. It had a hook screwed into one end which he used to unfasten the catches of the windows beneath the tall stained glass figures on the walls.

St. Bridget's floor plan resembled a cross. The long stem formed the back of the church. Then there were two alcoves beyond which lay the sanctuary. The windows along the main body of the church were traditional – St. Cecilia, St. Isidore, St. Elizabeth, and St. Patrick.

The windows in the alcoves attracted the most attention. While the charge has often been made since the Protestant Reformation that Catholics do not know or use their Bibles, the huge side windows were a hint that such was not the case. On the south side was a portrayal of the birth of Christ, a window that Fr. Ross loved to light from the outside with a spotlight at Christmas. Dimming the lights in the main body of the church made it the center of attention at the annual midnight Mass. The front wall contained a much smaller window of Isaiah, the prophet of Christmas.

The wall on the north side of the church had a large window depicting Adam and Eve being driven from the Garden of Eden. Its front window contained the figure of Elijah. Two smaller windows above the sanctuary contained Noah's Ark and images of Satan being cast from the heavens. In the back of church, above the choir loft, was a circular window with glass containing the image of St. Bridget. Born in Sweden in 1303, Bridget was praised by those who proclaimed her a visionary; denounced by the popes, cardinals, and rulers who were condemned by the content of such visions. They dismissed her as a religious nut.

The church was constructed of cream colored bricks that had been hauled by horse and wagon to the site over 100 years ago. St. Bridget's, under Fr. Ross' lead-ership, had celebrated its centennial two years before.

Having opened the windows, Fr. Ross stepped out-side to greet those who were arriving. On a summer night his own parishioners would be greatly out-num-bered by tourists. Fr. Ross still remembered his first summer at Wisconsin Dells. He had arrived on June 17, when the tourist season was beginning to peak. He never did get to know who his parishioners were until after Labor Day, when the crowds vanished and he was left with only townspeople.

The parishioners that Fr. Ross was greeting came from two distinctly different walks of life. Half owned or worked for the many amusements that clustered on either side of the bridge crossing the Wisconsin River.

Wisconsin Dells had begun its life as a narrow spot in the Wisconsin River with high sandstone banks where loggers risked their necks floating their wares through the swift and dangerous waters from the Northern for-ests to Southern sawmills.

According to the native Ho-Chunk Indians, the nar-rows had been formed thousands of years before when a giant bird had taken off in distant China and, as it flew eastward, had landed to rest on the icy regions of northern Canada. But the warmth of its heart began to melt the ice beneath it and slowly it began to slip down the side of the globe. Struggling to bring itself to a stop it reached out and tried to grasp the earth, but its claws tore away, leaving huge holes that became lakes. It beat its tail and tributaries to what would become the Wis-consin River, formed by the weight of its sliding body, came into existence. But then it came to a halt against a large rock mass. Waters, pushing from behind the beast, threatened to crush it. In a desperate effort to save its life, it gave a final lunge and broke through the rocks leaving behind it the Wisconsin Dells and its rock formations. But the great bird's surge was a final one. It dove deep into the earth leaving behind the bottom-less Devil's Lake surrounded by high rock cliffs.

It hadn't taken long for those who visited the area to discover the natural beauty of the rock formations that made up the banks of the river. Hotels catered to those who sought a scenic but quiet summer place.

In the 1970s and '80s water parks replaced the boat rides as the main attractions. River View, Noah's Ark, Family Land, and a number of smaller amusement parks vied for the tourist's dollar.

The other half of the parishioners came from the surrounding agricultural area. Many of the farms remained the original 160 acres that could be claimed under the Homestead Act. It was rolling land and the fields had been cut out of oak forests that still covered hills and valleys too steep to cultivate.

To the north, from Columbia County to Adams County, the land was sandy and difficult to grow crops on until the 1980s, when irrigation turned the territory into an area known as the golden sands where potatoes flourished and became a key source of income.

Still, many of the people remained poor. Poor, but proud. Few of the native people would accept or admit being on welfare.

Adams County could also claim another distinction. It had a reputation for violence. Periodically some crime would spill over into the Dells and surrounding counties, though this summer had been quiet. The only death that had been out of the ordinary was one that Fr. Ross had been involved in at St. Bridget's. A young parishioner had rolled his tractor over while working on a steep incline and had been crushed beneath it. Fr. Ross had been called to anoint the young farmer while he was still pinned beneath the tractor. Later he had conducted the funeral and continued to work with the widow and three children.

Fr. Ross stood facing the double doors of the church and welcomed those who came up its steps. The entrance was above the level of the sidewalk. Because St. Bridget's had been built close to the street, it was necessary to have the steps approach from both sides rather than straight from the front.

Among those attending the 5:30 p.m. Mass was Duke Lonergan. Duke had drifted into Fr. Ross's life upon the recommendation of friends when Fr. Ross, at the start of his pastorate, had been desperate for someone to care for the cemetery. The graves of the previous winter had to be covered with sod, the grass mowed, and bushes clipped. Memorial Day was approaching soon and Fr. Ross had known everyone would be aware of its condition.

Fr. Ross could still remember meeting with the bishop before coming to the parish. One of the things the bishop had shown him were photographs, sent to him by an irate parishioner, of the cemetery in a state of neglect. One photo contained the complaining letter writer lying in grass too tall to be seen. The bishop's order had been to clean it up. Duke had been Fr. Ross' answer to the problem.

Duke was retired, but he enjoyed working. Although he no longer drank, he had lost his family because of his drinking and the violence it caused. Now he lived alone in a rented trailer in the nearby town of Endeavor. He had come to the community seeking work in its single industry, a poultry processing plant. When it closed, he worked at a gas station. When the main highway was rerouted around Endeavor, he was again without work. That was when Fr. Ross had been introduced to him.

Lonergan's attire was always the same: blue denim work pants, plaid cotton shirt with a white T-shirt visible at its neck, high topped leather shoes laced through holes at the bottom and clips at the top, and a baseball cap bearing the logo of the giver. The present one was a gift of Dells Lumber.

His suntanned face bore the lines of age. Thin wisps of grey hair still could be found on his head. But his eyes revealed the spirit of youth. There were days when Fr. Ross felt the weight of the world bearing down on him only to look out a window and see Duke trimming a hedge, mowing lawn, or edging a sidewalk, and instantly cares seemed to vanish. Even if Duke had not been a good worker, which he was, he would have been worth having around.

"Good evening, Duke," Fr. Ross said as he spied him coming toward him.

Duke smiled instantly, happy to be recognized. He wasn't a member of St. Bridget's, much less Catholic, but he made the drive over because St. Bridget's was home. Having done all of the yard work around his trailer earlier in the day, a pervasive feeling of loneliness had prompted him to make the 15-mile drive to the Dells. Even if the conversation was short, it was a sign of being accepted. He could sense Fr. Ross's mysterious admiration for him, and this made up for a lack of family.

"Good evening," Duke returned as he moved up beside Fr. Ross and leaned against the cream-colored brick wall that was contoured to serve as a handrail on the side of the steps facing the street. In the midst of all his parishioners and their summer attire, Fr. Ross looked out of place in clerical black. He didn't always wear black, but he always wore a clerical collar during what he referred to as his business day. He defined business as anytime he was with the public. On weekends he always wore a sport coat, no matter how warm the weather. Duke wore a clean pair of denim work pants and a long-sleeved blue plaid shirt rolled up twice at the wrist as his only concession to summer.

The conversation made them oblivious to the rest of the people who walked by. When Fr. Ross glanced at his watch it was 5:20. The two parted and Fr. Ross stepped into the vestibule where he was met by the ushers, wearing red blazers. The ushers hated them because they were warm, but Fr. Ross wanted to impress guests who, on this night, far outnumbered parishioners.

Fr. Ross spoke to each one and then moved up the center aisle to the lectern on the left side of the sanctuary. He was proud of the lectern because he had designed it from the communion rail that had been taken down during the reforms of the Vatican Council.

The parish still remembered the days before Fr. Ross and the liturgical changes that they involved. An aged pastor had been sent a young assistant who was determined to make changes in a hurry in an effort to keep up with the latest decrees. When the pastor objected, the associate waited until he went on a two week vacation in Arizona for his health. Then the associate had a dump truck back up to the entrance of the church. He threw the communion rail, marble holy water founts, and numerous statues into the truck. He would have removed the tops of the tall center and main altars and left them as tables, but it was too big a task for one person, and no one would help him for fear of what would happen when the pastor returned.

Parishioners still remembered seeing the statue of St. Bridget perched precariously on top of the dump truck headed for the city landfill. When they recovered from the shock, the dump truck had already deposited its cargo, so a number of them went out and rescued what they held sacred.

The altar rail had gone to a farmer's machine shed; St. Bridget and her banished friends, including two angels from the main altar, found shelter in a garage; and the marble holy water founts became bird baths in a back yard. There they languished until Fr. Ross' centennial renovation.

Then the angels returned to their positions on either end of the main altar and the lanterns they held above their heads once again burned during the celebration of Mass. St. Bridget, after her damaged hands and face were repaired and she was repainted, took a place of prominence in the newly created baptismal area. Workers brought an old wood baptismal fount from storage, removed several coats of paint and placed one of the marble basins from the holy water founts in it to serve as the center of the baptismal area. Parts of the altar rail were used for newly built lecterns. Other parts were used around the baptismal area. Rather than pitch the past, Fr. Ross wanted to incorporate it into the present in a meaningful way.

From his place at the lectern, Fr. Ross made a few brief announcements, then continued on into the sacristy where he greeted the altar girls and vested for Mass. He prided himself in never having started a Mass late in his career as a priest.

"If you start five minutes late," he often told people, "the congregation will start coming five minutes late. If you are prompt, the people will be also."

Another personal rule was limiting his sermons to seven minutes. "If it can't be said in seven minutes, the preacher didn't prepare or didn't know what he wanted to say," he said. It was a rule he had often thought of having posted in the sacristy for visiting priests to study. How often he returned from a trip to the complaint, "Who was that priest? He talked for an hour!"

He always tried to say Mass in forty-five minutes. In that time everything could be done devoutly and still not try people's patience. He constantly had to remind song leaders and the choir, who thought nothing of dropping in another song and adding five minutes to the celebration, of his goal.

Fr. Ross was well within all of his rules on this Saturday evening. Forty minutes elapsed between the time he and the servers walked up the center aisle and then walked back out.

Those who had worshipped quickly dispersed, leaving Fr. Ross alone to put the sacred vessels away, turn off the lights, and lock the doors. After doing that, he made his way down the iron steps and walked to the side door of the rectory.

Fr. Ross loved Saturday nights for the solitude they brought. He often put a steak on the grill and a potato and some other vegetables in the microwave and enjoyed a sit-down meal. If it was summer, the meal would be preceded by a fresh salad made with ingredients supplied from parishioners' gardens. It had taken about four years, but he finally convinced his neighbors that he enjoyed such things much more than cookies and pies. It kept him trim and healthy. At the same time he was a fast food and deli expert, claiming that he ate better than half his meals standing up or in his 1984 Fiero in less than ten minutes. Life, Fr. Ross had found, was filled with contradictions.

His steak on this evening was a gift from the gracious winner of a half of beef in a parish drawing. His salad contained tomatoes, peppers, radishes, and a slice of onion. He washed it down with sparkling seltzer. Dessert would be a Snickers bar he would eat later in the evening.

What made Saturday evening so enjoyable was its flexibility. Fr. Ross would still do some work, but at his own pace, and that made it seem like recreation. After doing a few things at his desk, he would read, spend some time in meditation, and then go to bed.

It was while he was at his desk overlooking the street in front of the rectory that he noticed the newspaper clipping. Fr. Ross had a way of getting behind on his mail and often put aside those letters that he guessed were not official. He would open them later. He had once received a card from a person who apologized for not knowing when his birthday was, but was sure it was in the month of August. He responded by saying that was fine, because he hadn't opened his birthday cards until November. No need for an apology.

Such was the case now. He opened a letter from a classmate who was a priest in Roanoke, Virginia. It concerned a priest who had studied with them and become a military chaplain at Fort Rucker, Alabama.

Two newspaper articles were enclosed with the letter. The first described how a priest had been abducted from an airport while returning from a vacation. He had called the people he visited to assure them his flight had been a safe one. Then he vanished.

It was the second article, though, that would serve

as a constant distraction during Fr. Ross' meditation that evening. The car that the chaplain had been driving was found totally destroyed by fire. But even more mysteriously, the body of a man, burned beyond recognition, was discovered on what had been a pile of discarded lumber in a landfill. His hands and feet were tied, and he had been stabbed numerous times.

After the 5:30 Mass, Duke Lonergan drove to the north side of Wisconsin Dells to St. Bridget's cemetery. It was located on a hillside and he could have viewed it from the street, but chose instead to drive in through the red brick gateposts. He wanted to make sure that everything was as he had left it on Friday. Duke took pride in his work and he didn't want any parishioners finding something wrong and calling Fr. Ross.

Satisfied that everything was in order, he drove back out to the main street and headed east toward Endeavor on Highway 23. He was in no hurry, so he kept his old brown Delta 88 at a steady 45. The large Church of God Convention Center was on his left as he rounded a sweeping curve. Once a year, at the very end of the tourist season, its members filled the town for a weeklong gathering. Now its huge parking lot was empty.

In the rolling hills that followed was a green house with a number of outbuildings. Duke was convinced that the owners had a pet lion and had told Fr. Ross about it. Tonight he looked to see if the animal was visible, but could see nothing.

Briggsville lay halfway between Wisconsin Dells and Endeavor. It began as a mill town on the shores of Lake Mason. The seven-mile-long Lake Mason was created when the founders of the town erected a dam on the Neenah Creek as a source of power for their mill.

Duke decided to stop at the Cove, a restaurant on a

small inlet just outside Briggsville. He had stopped there after one of his first days at work at St. Bridget's and had gotten to know the owners, Chris and Caitlyn Walker, very well. In fact, he stopped there so often he was like family. It was so different from the old days when he could easily wear out a welcome on one Saturday night.

Fifteen years ago he would have ordered a beer before he got to the bar. That was no longer true. If Chris wasn't too busy behind the bar, he would take a seat and have a 7-Up before taking a table. If Chris was busy, he would walk down to the end of the bar where Caitlyn waited to seat dinner guests. During the summer months there was little time for long visits, but from the end of deer hunting season in November until April, when the summer residents and campers returned, there was always time for conversation. On those nights he and Chris often ate together. If Chris was busy, Caitlyn would come and sit for a while. Chris and Caitlyn enjoyed his company and even invited him over for a family dinner on Tuesday nights when the Cove was closed.

"Evening, Duke," Chris said as he saw Duke come through the door. He had gotten to know Duke's routine and had expected him.

Duke smiled as he sat on a stool and, with elbows on the bar, rested his chin for a moment on his crossed fingers.

"How's that dog doing?" asked Duke. Chris loved hunting and was busy training a Brittany for the fall partridge season.

"Had him out today, but I still haven't got him used to live birds," Chris said. "He'll retrieve a dummy with feathers tied on it, but as soon as I add quail scent, he won't pick it up. He's coming though. Want a 7-Up?"

Duke nodded and Chris moved down the bar to get it. The inside of the Cove had pine log walls. There was also a wall behind the bar that served as a divider between the bar and eating area. It was made of matching varnished pine logs with glass shelves for liquor above the counter that ran along it. An old-fashioned brass cash register sat in the center of the counter.

Chris returned with the 7-Up. "What's Fr. Ross doing this evening?"

"He's a good man," Duke said with a touch of admiration in his voice. "Seemed different tonight, though. His face tells what he's thinking. People always watch him at Mass, and every so often they catch him smiling. Then they know his mind is a million miles away, thinking of something funny that has happened. He wasn't smiling tonight, but he left the impression that he was thinking about something else. Something had to be going on that no one knew about. He is so tight-lipped, you'd never find out."

Chris moved to greet some customers who had just arrived. He had bought the business ten years before, after a not-so-successful stint as a farmer. It was obvious he loved it. He greeted every customer who came in and tried to get to know everyone. Even while he sat and ate with Duke, he kept one eye on what was happening in the restaurant and, at any moment, would get up and ask a waitress if certain things had been done. Was it time to take the salad dishes from that table? Was still another table waiting for its bill? Duke never said anything, but he was amused at an expression Chris used when checking to see if the water glasses had been filled at a certain table. Chris would ask the waitress to water a table. It always gave him the impression that animals were the subject of Chris' concern.

But it paid off, the restaurant was a success. On an average Friday night in the summer, the Cove could count on 450 guests, and that was pushing the limits.

Chris was quick to point out that the major reason the restaurant was a success was his wife, Caitlyn. She was waiting for him at the end of the bar and smiled as Duke slid off his stool and moved toward her. Like Chris, she was in her early forties. She wore her light red hair, which betrayed her Irish ancestry, cut short and straight. Duke often thought there was a great deal of fatigue hidden beneath her wide smile, especially during the summer months.

"Your favorite table is open," Caitlyn said with a grin. She knew he liked the small table that overlooked the inlet leading to the lake. "Kyla will be your waitress. May I bring you another 7-Up?"

Kyla, the Walker's oldest daughter, finished serving another table before getting to Duke. In the meantime Caitlyn brought Duke another 7-Up. Duke sat for a moment enjoying the warmth of the Walker's friendship. It might be a restaurant for others, but for Duke it had become a home, just as St. Bridget's had.

"Hi, Duke!" Kyla said, turning her order book to a new page. "Dad had some nice thick pork chops cut yesterday. I think he had you in mind."

"How quickly you've come to know an old man's habits," Duke answered. On Sunday evenings, he always ordered a mushroom burger. On Wednesdays he had the buffet and ate the ribs and a piece of beef with the vegetable. On other evenings he always had pork chops and a baked potato. "I'll have the pork chops and a baked potato with coffee a little later."

He settled back in silence to study the inlet as Kyla left to place his order. As well as the inlet one had a view of Lake Mason, which it opened out into, and Amey's Pond which was on the other side of the highway. Occasionally a boat sped across the horizon. One boat with two fishermen made its way slowly into the inlet and under the bridge on the way to Amey's Pond.

Duke ate his supper in silence, enjoying the view and the summer night. He said good night to Kyla as she brought his bill and left her a generous tip. Caitlyn was waiting at the cash register.

"It's not like winter, is it?" she said, referring to the lack of time to visit and knowing Duke missed it.

"No," said Duke, "but you couldn't pay the bills if it was." Chris had often told Duke that they could close the restaurant from January to April and not lose money.

The bar was crowded with customers, some still waiting to be served.

"Good night, Duke," Chris said as he mixed two brandy old fashions.

"Night," Duke replied putting his Dells Lumber cap on his head and moving toward the door.

The sun was beginning to set as Duke pulled out of the parking lot. "It'll be dark by the time I get home," he said to himself.

It was two miles from the Cove to Briggsville. Duke slowed at the edge of the town, which was two streets wide and six blocks long. It was split in half by the mill dam and the creek that disappeared into a marsh on the eastern side of the highway. The northern side had been settled by the Irish, and the farming territory beyond it was still known as the Irish Flats. The Germans had built to the south of the dam. In its early days, the school and post office had moved from side to side, depending on which nationality could command the majority vote at the polls. The village was about the same size it had been in the early 1900s.

The highway also served as the second street along the lake. As Duke drove, he glanced at the heart of town – O'Brien's Shell Station, The Pheasant Inn, Clark's Restaurant, and Kimball's Store. There had been another store, but it had closed and was now the Post Office. The building that had been a barbershop was still there, but had not been open since the death of its owner.

A green, single-story ranch house made Duke think of a story he had heard while working for Dairyland Poultry in Endeavor. He worked with the crew that caught chickens at night and many times, after the work was over, the boss's wife would have a meal waiting back at the plant. One beer would lead to another, one story to another. One night one of the old-timers had told the story of a past owner of that green house, which in its day was one of the most fashionable in the area.

The old man referred to the owner as Doc Hansen. Doc had known a young man was murdered but he had listed it as a heart attack.

Later, the undertaker had called Doc and asked him what he meant by saying it was a heart attack. There was a hole in the man's chest big enough to put a fist in. It was obvious he had been murdered. And most people assumed his wife had pulled the trigger.

"Could be," Doc said, "but he was a mean son of a bitch and I say it was a heart attack."

There were no more questions and the young man was buried without further investigation.

It was a story Duke had heard in the dark of night. Doc Hansen had died years before, and the story teller never revealed the names, so there was no way of knowing if the story was true or not.

The area between Briggsville and Endeavor was dotted with small farms. Driving a steady 45 mph Duke went under the new main highway that by-passed Endeavor. Then he turned onto the old highway that would take him into the town of 154 people. His trailer was on the north side of town.

Like most small towns in Wisconsin, Endeavor's business district suffered from the loss of a main highway, which now skirted it, and shopping malls that had gone up in the larger nearby cities. The three gas stations had closed. Only the grocery store, hardware store, and bank remained open in what had been a shopping district with five other stores, a meat market, and an implement dealership.

Tougher meat inspection laws that required the hiring of someone who was licensed to inspect meat processing had caused the owner of the meat market to close his doors. In the past, he had only sold his own meats, and slaughtered pigs and cows for local farmers.

Two elderly men had run the implement dealership and a Sinclair gas station and garage. People who worked at Dairyland Poultry would always remember

Ralph Parsons, who managed the station; Hank McCarthy sold Allis Chalmers machinery and parts from a large orange building across the street from the station. On Friday night Ralph cashed paychecks from a large roll of bills that he kept in the front of his silver and black striped bib overalls.

The town had been "dry" until the early 1960s, when voters permitted the opening of a tavern on its north side. "Old Hook" Glenn Turner was its first owner. It thrived in the days when the highway went right by it and Dairyland Poultry had 150 employees. "Old Hook" had sold it at its peak. Now it depended upon local residents for its trade, and Wisconsin's new, tough drunk driving laws cut into that market.

Turning left at the tavern, now known as Herman's, Duke drove two blocks west toward his small light blue trailer. It was dark when he brought the Delta 88 to a stop in the dirt driveway. He pushed the headlight knob off, climbed out of the car, and walked the short distance to the front door.

The trailer that he rented wasn't large. One room served as a kitchen and living room area. Behind that was a small bedroom, a bathroom, and a larger bedroom. A lady cleaned the house once a week, which was fortunate, because Duke was not the best of housekeepers. "Fr. Ross is always pleased with the way I mow lawns and trim hedges, but he always has something to say about my dusting," Duke would often say. In the summer Duke's responsibilities were cleaning the church and maintaining the cemetery. In the winter, when there was nothing to do in the cemetery, Fr. Ross would often have Duke help clean the school as a way for him to earn some spending money. Duke appreciated the work and the opportunity to be at St. Bridget's, but he hated the cleaning.

Duke, deciding that the ashtray on the coffee table could hold one more cigarette even though there were ashes surrounding it, sat down on the sofa to have another Salem while glancing at the newspaper. When he had smoked it down to the filter, he stubbed it out and went to bed.

Duke wasn't sure when he had the dream, but he knew that when he woke up he had looked out the window and there was no morning light. He would decide whether he should tell Fr. Ross about it some other time.

In the morning the memory of the dream was as clear as the dream itself. He had died, and he found himself part of a crowd rushing down a long passageway filled with the most brilliant light he had ever seen. At the end of the passageway he was confident he would enter into eternity.

He wasn't frightened. Everything seemed so peaceful. He looked at the others who were moving with him. They were dressed in white robes, but faceless.

As he neared the end of the passageway, there seemed to be a boundary separating him from countless white figures and golden buildings. He slowed, and as he did, a figure stepped out of the crowd beyond the boundary to greet him. Duke looked into the hood of the shining figure and recognized his father's face. Nothing had changed from Duke's last memories of him. His blue eyes sparkled and were filled with joy. The deep pores were still on his cheeks. His teeth were set evenly in his jaw and, except for a gold line on the base of one, were perfect. His face had the deep tan of late summer.

"Duke," his father said, "you have to go back."

But Duke didn't want to. He felt drawn toward the city of light and away from his old earthly dwelling. He moved on past his father.

Then two more figures came to meet him from the city beyond the horizon. Again, unlike the fellow travelers who were streaming by him on the way to the golden city, these also had faces. He recognized his dad's parents.

"You have to turn back," they said to him. "It isn't your time yet. You have a mission to do."

Reluctantly Duke turned to go back. As he was returning down the passageway, he could see white garmented people continuing to stream toward the eternal city. All around him were faceless people. Some proceeded toward the boundary that seemed to separate the eternal city from the earthly. Others, like him, were sadly returning to their earthly bodies.

Then Duke looked across at those going to the boundary.

Suddenly he made out a face coming toward him. It was Fr. Ross. Silently he moved by Duke.

3

"I alone remain," said the thin young man as he pointed at the Bible opened to the first book of Samuel. He spoke to no one, although his mother stood nearby and his father sat in a chair before a window.

"I alone remain, a prophet of the Lord; but the prophets of Baal are four hundred and fifty men."

"Why have you returned?" his mother asked as she tried to understand a son she no longer knew.

"Hear me, O Lord, hear me, that this people may learn," the young man spoke forcefully, but to no one in particular.

"Learn what?"

"Then the fire of the Lord fell and consumed the holocaust ...and when the people saw this, they fell on their faces."

Tears formed in the eyes of the elderly lady sitting at the table. Nothing she said could break through the rhetoric.

"And Elijah said, 'Take the prophets of Baal, and let not one of them escape...kill them.'

"And the hand of the Lord was upon Elijah!" Jim Elliot thundered as he picked his Bible off the table and disappeared in the direction of his bedroom.

Krista Elliot listened to the pounding of feet going upstairs and then down the hall. She cried and wiped the tears away with the dishtowel she had twisted in her hands during her son's ramblings.

It didn't make sense. Krista had been so happy when she saw Jim step unexpectedly from an old, battered Chevrolet three days before. He had been gone more than three years, leaving without explanation and now returning without explanation.

Previous to his leaving, neighbors had seen him sitting by himself in his red Camaro on deserted side roads at odd hours of the day. Months later she heard a rumor that he had been in a fight at work and had claimed to be Jesus Christ.

The night before his mysterious departure Jim may have been giving her a clue, but it was one that she had missed the significance of until after he left. She was working in the garden when he drove into the yard that night. He was proud of his car and she found nothing strange about the fact that he had washed it. When he finished, he came over to the edge of the garden. He spoke not about his work but about going to the library. Then he said that he wouldn't be helping her with the garden and walked back toward the house. Krista thought he meant helping in the garden that night. It was only later that she began to realize it foreshadowed a decision about the future.

Krista was accustomed to her son's unexplained absences for several days at a time. But this time, weeks went by. Beginning to worry, she called the store where he was employed in Chicago. When Jim hadn't come in for work, his employer assumed he had walked off the job. He had been warned about unexcused absences in the past and it was just a matter of time before Jim would have been fired anyway.

Krista didn't notify the police. She assumed that they would be too busy with everything else that was happening during the summer in Wisconsin Dells to be bothered about a twenty-six-year-old man who would probably show up on his own in the future. Besides, it was difficult for her to get into town. She couldn't drive, and her husband, Ed, had lost the ability to do so. The only time she left the farm house was when a neighbor, Bernice Evans, stopped by to pick her up for the 10 a.m. Mass at St. Bridget's or to take her shopping. Then her husband complained about her being gone.

"He'll show up," Ed Elliot answered gruffly when his wife voiced her concern. "He's been gone before. He always came back. It's nobody else's business. Besides, if you go talking to the police, we'll soon have them and the game wardens out here." Ed was an old game violator who tried to avoid any law enforcement for fear of being found out.

Then, on a warm day in June as Krista was walking from the garden to her kitchen, she saw a car approaching along the long, dusty driveway. She stopped, wondering who it might be. She had always hoped that a shiny red Camaro would appear. This car was red, but old and unkempt. Jim had always been meticulous. Dust never settled on his car.

It seemed strange when the car parked on the grass under the tree where Jim had always parked. There was a pause, and then the driver's door opened. Her heart stopped when a head appeared above the roof line.

"Jim!"

"Jim! Is that you?" Excited, she wanted to run, but arthritis kept her from doing so. The one bright spot in her dismal life had returned. Her faded blue eyes sparkled for the first time in three years.

"Jim!" Krista shouted joyfully as she hobbled toward him. When she reached him, she threw her arms around him. The one person she loved, the one person who gave her hope had returned.

But Jim reacted with indifference. Crushed and confused, she realized Jim had changed. He was no longer the son who loved her and had watched over her.

In the past he spoke with pride about his and his parents' ability to be self sufficient in the face of poverty. They managed, during the hard times, by hunting and fishing in season and out.

"My father had a Winchester .22 pump action rifle that

could be taken apart and concealed in two long pockets that Mom had sewn in his heavy coat. When we really got hungry, Dad would walk out the door with that gun hidden in his coat. Soon there was venison to eat."

While other grade school children bragged about their fathers' business accomplishments, Jim always talked about the days his father had been an amateur boxer and how they still relived those days as they went to a nearby tavern and watched the Friday night fights. Jim knew boxers' records in the same fashion as his peers knew baseball players and batting averages. He enjoyed being admired for that knowledge.

Jim also bragged about his father's ability to fish. When classmates came to visit him, he would get his father to tell the story of the giant fish in Ennis Lake. "It was evening, and I was using a cane pole and a minnow," Ed would say as he ran through the lines of an often-repeated story. "When that fish hit, I could tell it was a big one. I was afraid it would break the line or the pole, so I threw the pole overboard and let the fish tire itself out pulling the pole around. I just kept rowing after the pole until the fish was exhausted." Ed would pause to pick up an empty Maxwell House coffee can that served as his spittoon and, after a much practiced spit, conclude, "It was the largest northern pike ever caught in Ennis Lake."

But Ed had grown old, and by the time Jim was in high school, he had become the provider, while his father spent most of his time sitting in a wooden rocking chair and looking out a picture window at the woods he had once hunted in.

Jim was proud of his father and proud to be taking his place as the one who kept food on the table. His mom and dad never had new clothes. The owner of the house often let the rent slide in a spirit of charity. But there was always food on the table: in the fall Jim hunted, and in the summer hardly a night went by that he didn't go fishing in one of several small lakes nearby.

One summer night he confided to a fishing partner, "I catch enough fish to keep us from having to buy meat. My mom grows everything else in the garden."

While other boys his age were buying bicycles, Jim had his own fourteen-foot aluminum fishing boat and a motor he had repaired after a neighbor had thrown it out as junk. He was skilled in handling boats by the time he was fourteen and often volunteered to man the motor for anyone who would take him fishing. One of his greatest moments had been when a former teacher, feeling sorry for Jim's poor state in life but knowing his great love for fishing, had taken him out on Lake Michigan fishing for trout and coho. The teacher had even let Jim take control of the cabin cruiser and was amazed at his ability to keep it on course in rough waters.

But now, for some unknown reason, Jim had changed. His father was no longer a hero.

Jim came running into the kitchen with the Bible in his hand.

"You drank away any chance we had for a decent life," Jim screamed at his father.

"You weren't a boxer, just a barroom brawler. Lies! Lies! You lied to me! You were just a bum and I had to lie to cover for you.

"Hear me, O Lord, that this people may learn!"

Ed had no defense. He sat in his rocking chair and looked out the window. His left hand, twisted and hardened into a set position, as a result of being caught in the rollers of a corn shredder, rested on the well-worn arm of the chair. His right hand held his makeshift spittoon. Bib overalls covered a stomach too large for a five-eight frame. Age and lack of understanding robbed his face of emotion. His blue eyes stared vacantly into the countryside beyond the window. Ed knew no other reaction than, for the moment, to be silent.

Finishing his attack on his father, Jim jerked one of the wooden chairs from its place at the kitchen table. He sat down across from his mother and placed his Bible on the worn oil cloth.

"I am alone!" He said.

Jim paused to open the Bible.

"But I have been chosen by the Lord," he said, raising a crooked finger that might have belonged to any prophet of old beseeching his listeners.

"I was born on July third. July is the seventh month. Three is a holy number. Seven. Three." Jim repeated the numbers.

"When I was up in my room I saw the prophets of Baal."

"You saw nothing. There was no one up there," Krista whispered.

More than a correction, it was a statement of belief. Jim observed it and shot back, "Oh yes, they were there. I could see them hiding among the flowers on the wallpaper. The prophets of Baal. They wanted to come out and attack me, but the power of God was with me. They knew I could call down fire and have them destroyed, so they hid behind the flowers, but I saw them."

Jim closed his Bible and, giving his mother a knowing look, pushed his chair back from the table.

"They were there. I heard them cursing me," he said as he rose and left.

Krista watched him through the screen door. She could hear his voice repeating the message of the prophets of Baal as he walked toward the barn and disappeared in the woods behind it.

Bewildered, she fixed her gaze on the empty wood burning stove that sat on a sheet of galvanized metal in the corner of the room. "Jim, Jim, Jim," she whispered in anguish. "Come back."

There seemed to be no way to talk sense to him, to break through the words he hurled about.

Her eyes shifted to the yellowed picture of the Sacred Heart hanging on the wall near the stove. Jesus, standing, pointing to his heart, which was wrapped in thorns. There seemed to be a special sorrow in his eyes. She could identify with the sorrow and the thorns piercing his heart. Her own heart ached. Tears filled her eyes as she prayed. "Lord, please help Jim. Make him who he used to be. Give him back his mind. Help him get his mind clear. He is all I have in this life. There hasn't been much in this life. A bad choice. A husband who drank. Little money. But You gave me him and that made up for it all. He was doing so well until that year before he left. Those were good times and I was so proud of him. If I didn't have anything else, I had him. I have loved him so.

"I prayed so much for his return and was so happy to see that face again, but he is a different person. The sparkle is gone from his eyes, the love from his heart. He is no longer mine."

Ed interrupted her prayer. "He shouldn't have returned if he's going to talk like that, should have stayed where he was."

"No. I'm glad he came back," Krista said patiently. It was difficult enough dealing with Jim without having her husband get involved.

"He's no good to us. I can't do anything. My legs just won't let me get around anymore. Look at him. Gone. Now that he's back all he does is wave that Bible and talk crazy." Ed stopped talking to spit in the Maxwell House can.

Krista went to the sink and took a white dishpan from the shelf beside it. She could still hear Ed as she escaped to the garden. There was no use trying to explain it — she didn't understand it herself. She needed time to think and there were peas to pick. When the task was over, she stopped at the end of the row to sit and rest on a wooden chair that had the back cut off. She looked at the scrub oak trees behind the barn. There was no sign of her son. She wondered if he would return for dinner. He always loved those woods. Maybe it would change him.

When she returned to the house, she shucked and washed the peas. Dinner would be peas, potatoes, bread, and pieces of a roast that had been stored in the refrigerator. Unsure whether or not Jim would emerge from the woods, she set a third place. She carefully placed the plain white dishes and coffee cups on the table and, beside the plates, put unadorned heavy handled knives and forks. She left the spoons in a cup at the center of the table, to be used as needed.

Ed and Krista were sitting at the table when Jim entered the house. He walked by them and went upstairs without looking at either.

Krista got up and went to the stairs. "Jim, come and eat," she said.

She was already in her chair at the table by the time Jim came down and took his place. He put his Bible on the table beside him and began to eat.

No one spoke. Krista was worried about what Ed might say. She searched for the right words to say.

Jim wiped a piece of bread across his plate and was still chewing it when he began to talk.

"The devil is in my room. I saw him on the wallpaper. His breath was like fire. He threatened to kill me. I've got to go to church. It is the only place I can be safe. Devils can't go in church."

Jim rose from the table and ran to the door. His mother heard the old red Chevrolet grind to a start. She walked to the front room and watched as it disappeared down the long driveway, leaving a thin cloud of dust behind it. The car paused at the highway and then turned in the direction of Wisconsin Dells.

4

Fr. Ross' eyes were blurred with sleep as he answered the door at 3 a.m. He opened the door a crack. The figure outside shoved it open and dashed inside before he had time to react.

"I just saw the devil and I grabbed Jesus and ran," the young lady exclaimed, reaching beneath her blouse to pull a small corpus of Christ from the cup of her bra.

How did she get in that quickly, Fr. Ross asked himself, his mind still clearing. Once it got dark he never let strangers in the house, preferring to meet with them on the front steps. He had many unexpected calls while alone in the rectory at night and experience had taught him not everyone could be trusted. One evening a young man called to speak to a priest, explaining he was a stranger attending a nearby Diesel driving school for a week and needed to talk right away. Fr. Ross agreed to meet him under a street light across from the police station. An excellent site, Fr. Ross decided as he noticed the knife sticking out of the man's boot top and heard him talk about a girlfriend who had jilted him and moved to Alabama. "Maybe I should go and kill the guy who took her there and bring her back," the man had threatened.

Now Fr. Ross had a problem. If he told the woman to get out or helped her out, she might start screaming accusations that would be heard by neighbors. How would he explain it? There really wasn't anything to do but hear her out.

"Why don't you come in the office?" he asked as he walked by her and switched on the light to the adjoining room. She followed him but refused to sit down.

"Get me a jacket," she said as she paced the floor in front of his desk. Spotting one on a chair, she grabbed it and knelt to brace it up in a corner. "The devil was in my jacket! The arms kept puffing up and I could see his face in the hood!"

Abandoning the jacket, she got to her feet, pulled the chair up to the front of his desk, and sat down. As quickly as she had sat down she jumped up and went over to kneel by the jacket. "The devil was in my jacket!" she repeated as she fluffed the jacket. "The arms kept puffing up and I could see his face in the hood."

Again the young lady stood up, this time fishing a pack of cigarettes and butane lighter from the pockets of her blue jeans. Without asking, she lit up a cigarette. Fr. Ross pulled an ashtray from a drawer and placed it on the desk in front of her.

"What is your name?" he asked, hoping to establish some semblance of order.

"Barbara McNulty," replied the woman who was now seated across from him.

"I don't think I have seen you before. Are you a member of this parish?"

"No, I can't go to church. I'm single and all those people in your church are couples. I can't go there!"

Slowly the face began to register in Fr. Ross' memory. Fr. Clark, the chaplain at the Baraboo Hospital, had met him in the hospital corridors as he was making his weekly visits and told him of a young lady from his town, Barbara McNulty. Fr. Ross was not familiar with the name, but decided to call on the patient anyway. It wasn't much of a visit as a nurse was in the room and he had only been permitted to introduce himself. Evidently that introduction had brought this woman to the rectory in the middle of the night.

"I grabbed Jesus and ran," Barbara said as she laid the small figure of Christ, that had been detached from a crucifix, on the desk before her. Then she rose and once again made her way to the corner where she had placed the jacket.

"I saw him," Barbara said, holding the jacket before her. "His face was in the hood." She put the jacket down and again returned to the chair.

Fr. Ross glanced at his watch. It was three fifteen. He knew it would be some time before the woman would leave. She had to be high on something.

Barbara stubbed out the cigarette she was smoking and lit another one.

"I renounced Christ about two weeks ago," she said. "I said I was going to if I lost the man I was going with. I've had two abortions. The trouble is I have always given love too freely!"

"God is forgiving," Fr. Ross interjected. "Sometimes He is the person we have to turn to when we hit rock bottom."

"I saw the devil," said Barbara as she jumped up and knelt by the coat. As she braced it in the corner she repeated, "His face was in the hood."

She came back to the desk and attempted to stub her half- smoked cigarette out, but it broke in the middle. Leaving it to smolder, she flipped another one loose from the pack and raised the yellow Bic's flame toward it.

"I looked at a picture of Jesus and the heart was moving. It was as if it was alive."

"Palpitating," Fr. Ross suggested. There was little he could do, but let Barbara talk herself out.

Two hours went by; Barbara finally rose to leave.

"I'm not smoking dope. I'm not on coke," she reassured Fr. Ross as she left. "I had four beers. That's all."

After she left Fr. Ross returned to his desk. The room was filled with smoke. The jacket was still in the corner. The lighter was still on the desk, but the cigarettes and figure of Christ were gone. It was five-thirty in the morning, and he knew he wouldn't go back to sleep, so he decided to wash and shave and get ready for a day that already had an interesting start.

The extra time permitted Fr. Ross to read his breviary. Composed of various psalms, it was to be the official daily prayer for priests around the world. As a seminarian Fr. Ross had been taught that it was a sin not to say its proscribed prayers for each day. He could remember professors telling about times that they had stopped the car to read it under the dome light rather than risk sin. Fr. Ross had followed the church's admonition for several years, carrying the black prayer book with him and squeezing the prayers in at any available moment. But as time went on, he had stopped having it as a constant companion and often found himself substituting other prayers in its place. Still, he liked to go back to it. He always said it during Lent. Someday it would again become a year-round habit.

It was Wednesday morning, the final day of school, and he would be celebrating Mass with the grade school students. Cancellations due to snow had added some extra days to the school year, taking it beyond Memorial Day and into the month of June. Fr. Ross enjoyed the students and the Mondays and Wednesdays he spent each week teaching them and saying Mass with them.

Each morning, after a quick breakfast of coffee and toast, he would go to his card file and pull sermon material appropriate for the day's readings and those gathered. If a saint's day was being celebrated, he was careful to make note of it, especially if the students were there. "Kids need heroes and none could be better than those of the church. Modern heroes might prove to have feet of clay, but not these people," he often told others.

"Well, almost." Then he would caution women about St. Albert the Great. "It is said that he referred to women as misfits of nature and faulty men with less intelligence." The feast on this day offered no such difficulty. It was the feast of St. Justin, who had been beheaded in Rome in 165.

This day was special, the last day of school. He wished to thank the staff for their quality work. Fr. Ross believed he had the best that could be assembled. He wanted to tell the students to enjoy a safe summer and enjoy being young. One day he had watched two carefree fourth-grade boys ride their bicycles to school in the rain. He would tell them to go out and ride their bikes in the rain, fish, swim, and take advantage of their freedom. In the words of St. Paul, do the things of a child, because the day will come when you are no longer a child.

The servers, girls on this particular day, were already in the sacristy when he arrived. Students filed in as he walked out to the altar and lectern and arranged the books. He returned to the sacristy and placed enough hosts in the ciborium for the day's communicants and then took his own chalice out of its box and prepared it for Mass. The servers placed it on a small table in the sanctuary and returned for the start of Mass.

As he genuflected and stood behind the altar Fr. Ross glanced at the morning's crowd. There were only two people that Fr. Ross did not know, one a young man who sat near the back of church and the other a lady who had obviously accompanied Mrs. Colby. Arlene Colby was the outspoken traditionalist of the parish who was forever keeping check on whether or not the pastor was abiding by church norms, especially those of the pre-Vatican era. She would never think of entering church without a hat or doily pinned on her head. She knelt when others sat, sat when others stood, and did her best to continue the ritual of the old Latin Mass.

Frequently she would tell Fr. Ross of her visits to nearby Necedah, Wisconsin, and the shrine of the Blessed Mother. Known for its founder, Mrs. Van Hoof, it had been declared a hoax by the bishop and her followers were not to receive the sacraments in the surrounding Catholic churches unless they recanted. Mrs. Van Hoof had retaliated by finding her own priests, most of them, including one supposed Pope from Canada, clergy who had been ousted from other dioceses.

Fr. Ross knew Arlene was a follower of Mrs. Van Hoof's and that her children had received such sacraments as baptism and first communion from some of Van Hoof's priest friends, who still said Mass in Latin and considered themselves traditionalists. Still, he never banned her from going to communion at St. Bridget's. He considered her faith to be simple and he enjoyed from time to time the traditionalist criticism aimed at him.

What he wasn't prepared for was a voice coming from the line of people going to communion that would continue to repeat, "God forgive you." The speaker was hidden among the adults, who always received communion after the children who were seated in the front pews. As Arlene received and turned to walk away, Fr. Ross stood face to face with her friend. As he raised the host to her tongue, no traditionalist would receive Christ in their hand, the voice said for a final time, "God forgive you."

"He already has," responded Fr. Ross before giving her communion.

When Mass was over the friend, forgetting that in pre-Vatican days lay people were never permitted in the sanctuary, made her way to the sacristy. Fr. Ross was quick to dismiss the servers. There was no need for them to be caught up in a conversation they would never understand.

"Fr. Ross, I am visiting Mrs. Colby from Chicago."

No doubt both have been to Necedah the past weekend, Fr. Ross thought to himself.

"You have a wonderful church. I am impressed by the windows and the fact that you have the statues and old altars."

"We have just remodeled and tried as hard as we could to retain the things of the past."

"But Father, you let a woman help distribute communion and had girl servers. You must get rid of them."

"The Pope has approved them."

"I doubt very much if the Pope even knows this is going on. I am sure some liberal priest has put out this so-called approval without ever conferring with the Pope. I am going to write to the Pope and inform him of this American heresy. People like myself and Mrs. Colby have to be watch dogs."

"I am sure the Pope has more to do than be concerned about lay ministers and servers in this parish. Besides, women have always been welcome to actively participate in such ministries in any parish I have been a pastor in. I just feel their time has come."

"I can't agree with you. What kind of priest are you?"

"I work as hard as I can and I will let God be the judge. If the Pope says women may be involved in these activities I feel free to let them."

"But I really don't approve of women doing these things. I would never receive communion from anyone but a priest, not even a man. I consider what the church has done recently a disgrace."

"You are entitled to your own opinion, but I accept it.

Remember in the gospel when the disciples came running to Jesus with the news that someone was preaching in his name but wasn't a card carrying follower? Our Lord told them to forget it, that some good would come from it. There is some good in what all of us say, so don't be too quick to condemn. I'm sorry I can't talk any longer, but my students are expecting me at school."

Fr. Ross moved to the switch box, turned off the lights, and glanced out into the main body of the church. Kneeling in the front pew, within earshot of the conversation, was the young man who had knelt in back throughout Mass. He held a Bible in his hand and he read it as Fr. Ross looked at him. Perhaps he is one of the many vacationers, Fr. Ross thought to himself. Behind schedule, he left Arlene's nameless friend standing in the sacristy and walked out the door. As he walked down the black iron steps, he caught sight of Duke Lonergan replacing the candles that had burned out in the outdoor shrine to the Blessed Mother. It stood between the church and the rectory.

"Morning, Duke!"

"Morning," Duke replied. He would have been disappointed if Fr. Ross had not said anything, in fact, he chose to replace the candles at a time when he knew Fr. Ross would pass by.

"Ever hear of a gal named Barbara McNulty?"

Duke paused. The fact that Fr. Ross might know her puzzled him. He tried to think of a connection as he answered and couldn't.

"I doubt if you'll ever see her in church, Father," Duke said. "Barbara's got quite a reputation. They say she takes the last male customer home at whatever bar she ends up in. Does dope. Why do you ask?"

"Just wondering."

Tight-lipped as ever, Duke thought as he watched Fr. Ross walk toward the school. "Just wondering," was Fr. Ross' way of saying he was looking for some information but wasn't about to divulge any. Duke turned back toward the candle stands that were a part of the shrine.

Fr. Ross walked across the street to St. Bridget's School. The candles were supposed to burn for seven days, but even with a protective top over the glass globe the wind often blew them out. When that happened, Duke discarded them rather than lighting them again, although he often wondered what God thought about his cutting the prayer intention of someone else short.

St. Bridget's cream-colored brick school had been built prior to the Vatican Council, when the future of Catholic education seemed without limits. It had two floors, one above and one below street level. The lower level was accessible from the back, because the school had been dug into a natural incline. As one entered the upper lobby, the office was to the right. A gym, which stood over a large lunchroom, lay straight ahead. Wings to the left of the gym and lunchroom held classrooms. A tunnel beneath the street allowed students to cross from school to church, protected from winter cold and rain storms.

In post-Vatican years St. Bridget's had lost the religious order that had taught in it since its construction. The number of vocations had declined dramatically and the order had to pull back. Its 254 students were now served by a lay principal and teaching staff.

"The sacrifices they make in terms of lower wages and lost benefits are heroic," Fr. Ross would often remind his congregation and parish council when the annual discussion of wages came up. Although he knew the tremendous burden placed upon the parish, when it came to raising the money for their wages he felt deeply that they should always be treated with justice. If it was not possible, then the school should be discontinued.

Hands shot up as Fr. Ross entered the first-grade room. Soon the students were gathered around him.

"Will you guess my dog?"

"Will you guess my cat that has been dead for a month?"

"Will you guess my aunt's baby?"

"Can Joe and I go get the crystal ball?"

The teacher left the room, but only after commenting that the students knew they were not to leave their desks and comparing Fr. Ross to the Pied Piper.

Although Fr. Ross handed out report cards each quarter, he never looked at grades, because he wanted students to feel equal in his eyes. He also never permitted teachers to remain in the room during his half-hour visits each week. "It gives the students the freedom to say whatever they want," he concluded. And they usually did. "Besides, my class is a break from the grind."

As a result, classes were a mixture of religion, the crystal ball, amazing stories, the Tunnel Monster, and wrestling moves. The topic was dependent on the age level and interests of the students.

Pleading ignorance, Fr. Ross often had the lower grade boys demonstrating wrestling moves, such as brain busters and DDTs, on a giant Teddy Bear, that, like the crystal ball, was dragged from room to room. Once Fr. Ross had been embarrassed when a teacher walked back into the room, only to see a student standing on a desk about to demonstrate an earthquake on the Teddy Bear.

Fr. Ross entertained the first and second grades with his crystal ball, an old street light into which he would peer with his special glasses, and describe students' pets. He usually got a description of the animal from an older brother or parent after Mass the weekend before. Many times he could remember the pet from a home visit or from his annual pet blessing on the feast of St. Francis of Assisi. For the young student, it remained a mystery of magical proportions.

Fr. Ross was famous among his students for his stories about the Tunnel Monster that lived behind the school in the dumpster. It had a pointed head, one eye in the middle of its head, and a breath of fire, as well as eight octopus tentacles with suction cups on the ends. To look it in the eye was to be frozen in place. It could burn one to an ash at a distance of twenty feet with its

fiery breath. The long tentacles were capable of reaching out and lifting a car off the ground or attaching themselves to a forehead and dragging the victim into the
tunnels beneath the school or back into the dumpster.
Of course, it was always a student in the class who was
the victim and other students who came to the rescue.
Students begged to have parts in what had become an
on-going serial.

Teachers often returned at the end of the half-hour
to see students' hands raised in an attempt to tell one
last amazing story from their personal lives. A classic
was Sam's birthday party. Sam lived on a farm in the
country near a creek. While he was in fourth grade, his
birthday had fallen on a cold November day. Oblivious
to the weather, he and his guests had a mud fight that
ended with a skinny dip in the creek. Fr. Ross had
pledged not to tell any of the parents. Teachers were
happy when recess followed Fr. Ross' class. It gave students a chance to burn off energy generated during the
half-hour. "Never will I forget the new teacher who tried
a silent reading period after one of my classes. She only
tried it once. Religion is important, and I do teach a
surprising amount of it," he would say in defense of
himself, "but religion should also be fun. I want to leave
students with that impression. Impressions are often
more important than dry facts."

Having finished his final three classes for the year Fr.
Ross walked back down the corridor and out the front
door. He was surprised to see the young man who had
been at Mass standing near the shrine to the Blessed
Mother, the Lady of the Dells, obviously waiting for him.

As Fr. Ross crossed the street and stepped up on the
sidewalk in front of the shrine, the young man approached him.

"Good morning, Father."

"Good morning." Fr. Ross noticed the young man still
had the Bible in his hand. He also noted that he was
missing a front tooth and his face showed signs of
stress. But stress on the part of those who sought him

out was nothing unusual. It was his vocation to try, with a message of hope, to relieve some of it.

"Is there some way I can help you?" he asked the man, who wore blue jeans and a faded maroon T-shirt. There were dark circles under the pale blue eyes that seemed to look at him without focusing.

"I heard you talking to the lady after Mass this morning. I spoke to her after you left and she was very upset. She said you couldn't be a true priest of God."

"You have to understand whom it was you were talking to. Unfortunately, she belongs to a group of people who have never accepted the changes that the Pope himself has approved of. In fact, the bishop has said that unless they change their ways, they are not supposed to receive the sacraments."

"I just want to make sure you are a true priest. I need the counseling of our Father's holiest men. I need protection from doctors. They have tried to force me to take medicine, but I want to keep my body pure for God. I cannot make one mistake with Our Father's precious gift of life."

"I don't know if I am the holiest of men..."

"But I can come and talk to you? I need the protection of God's holiest men."

"Everyone is free to talk to me. You can always call or stop by." Fr. Ross didn't know if he would be able to help the young man, but he knew from experience that being a good listener was often enough. In fact, he had found that he would often be thanked after a session in which he felt bad about contributing very little. But he had listened.

"I have to go. I applied for a job in the Dells and I will be interviewed this morning. I'm a military veteran so I won't have any trouble getting it. But I want to make a covenant with the Lord."

There was something familiar about the voice, but as at Mass Fr. Ross could not place the individual who had not introduced himself. As the young man walked toward the downtown area of Wisconsin Dells, Fr. Ross glanced at his watch. He would have to hurry to be on time for his weekly Mass at the local nursing home. He quickly got his alb and Mass kit from the sacristy and walked to the garage, which was behind the house.

The drive to Continental Manor was a short one. The nursing home was located on the edge of town. Each week the social director gathered about twenty patients, some Catholic and some not, for his late morning Mass. Some walked, but most were wheeled in. There would be others who were confined to their rooms. He would take communion to them after he concluded Mass.

As he entered the lobby, a voice cried out, "Help me!" There was a pause and then, as if the voice operated at timed intervals, "Help me!"

"Morning, Martha," Fr. Ross said mildly.

"Help me," Martha said, addressing no one in particular. She was but one of a number of patients sitting in wheelchairs around the central desk area.

The community hall was to the left of the front lobby. As Fr. Ross entered, he greeted everyone in a loud and cheery voice. He hesitated at the wheelchair of Walter Reitz and studied the top of his head.

"Walter! I see three new hairs!"

Those who were capable of doing so laughed.

"Hey, look at Blanche," Fr. Ross said as he continued down the aisle between the wheelchairs. "Is that a new lap warmer? It looks beautiful."

Blanche explained that it was a birthday gift from her daughter.

A table served as an altar. As Fr. Ross prepared it for Mass and put his vestments on, he continued to be a source of entertainment. Marion Welsh, who had suffered for a year with cancer, sat in a wheelchair directly ahead of him. Fr. Ross had visited her in her home on his weekly communion call rounds for months before she moved to the nursing home. He enjoyed her pluckiness and ever-present smile in the face of adversity.

Marion had lost her hair during treatment and wore a night cap. Fr. Ross always noticed the color.

"I don't know if I have ever seen anyone with lavender hair. You must be going dancing tonight!"

"Oh, Father," Marion said, pleased at the attention he was giving her.

For Fr. Ross it was easy attention to give. Of all the people gathered in the room, she was the only one with cancer. From past experience, Fr. Ross knew what lay ahead, and anything he could do to make her life more cheerful in these final months he would do. He knew that somewhere in the future, as the pain became more intense, she would turn to him from her bed and say "I must have done something terribly wrong in my life for God to let this happen to me."

At that point Fr. Ross would have to search for words and meaning himself and assure her that her place in heaven would be higher than his was ever going to be. Then he would have to make those visits and watch her steady decline. It hurt not to be able to reach out and do something to raise her back to health again. He knew there would be that final time, perhaps in the middle of the night, when he would be called to her bedside by relatives.

Fr. Ross found it easy to give his attention to Marion Welsh. Her courage was that of a saint. Her final struggle would assure her of being one. Fr. Ross could only reflect on the power of healing given to the early Apostles, in the book of Acts those placed in the passing shadow of Peter and his companions were often cured. Fr. Ross regretted that the same power had never been bestowed on him. If only it would happen just once and he could witness the joy of the person cured.

By the end of the gospel a number of the patients gathered in the warm room were asleep. It was quite a contrast with the rooms full of energetic students he had just left. At the handshake of peace, Fr. Ross walked about the room and greeted each one. Some recognized him; some did not. Some could shake hands. Others, hands bent with arthritis, could only look at him and wait for his touch.

At the back of the room Elizabeth Bartol looked up at him from her chair. Grasping his hand, the one-hundred-two-year-old lady who always shuffled in on her own, said loud enough for all to hear, "I'll pray for you, Father."

Fr. Ross stopped. "You have a lot in common with St. Anthony of the Desert, Elizabeth. He lived to be one-hundred-five!"

"I don't feel well, Father. I think I'll go to my room after Mass and die."

Again, the residents laughed. Elizabeth had outlived many of the patients who had come to the Manor and they all presumed she would outlive them.

Having their attention, Fr. Ross surveyed the nodding heads from the back of the room and joked, "I think I may go back to the rectory and take a nap after this Mass. You are putting me in the mood for it."

"That's OK," the man with the bald head responded. "But don't go to sleep before you're done saying Mass!"

Smiling at the wit of the man, Fr. Ross returned to the altar and distributed communion. At the conclusion of Mass he visited rooms and then returned to gather up his Mass kit and say a few last words to those who had yet to be wheeled to the lunch room.

On his way back to the rectory Fr. Ross detoured to the north side of town and the cemetery. He drove through the red brick pillars that marked the entrance. The newest section of the cemetery lay closest to the street. Most of the graves were located on the hilltop.

Fr. Ross found Duke trimming around the headstones at the very top of the hill.

"Sure is different from before Memorial Day, isn't it Duke?"

"Definitely."

Before Memorial Day there had been cars and people in the cemetery from daybreak to dark, but now there was only an occasional visitor.

"We've got to look for a couple of graves. Jim Weber's second wife has decided that when she dies she wants Jim beside her. From what I understand she even took the matter to a lawyer, and it was approved, so he is going to be moved from beside his first wife to her plot." Duke raised his Dells Lumber hat and scratched the few white hairs that remained. "The guy has still got women chasing him and he's dead. Now that's something!"

Fr. Ross smiled as they began to walk toward the areas where he thought, from looking at the map beforehand, the graves would be located.

"Now, when I die I want to be cremated and have my ashes dumped over Buffalo Lake," Duke said. Buffalo Lake was a wide expanse of the Fox River which flowed by Endeavor. It was bordered by yards of cattails and had a muddy bottom that was continually stirred by carp. Duke always jokingly said a few more ashes sprinkled from above could hardly be considered contamination.

"Did I ever tell you about the time my buddy, Smokie, and I went duck hunting out there? Even though his poultry processing plant isn't in operation anymore he hasn't given up building what he calls his road to paradise through the cattails to where the ducks are. This one morning when the temperature was about twenty degrees we went out on the road to paradise. We had rowed out from its end and were just putting the decoys out when I looked down and saw water coming through the bottom of the boat."

"The boat's sinking!" I yelled to him.

"It sank, and we were standing up to our waists in freezing water. We couldn't get out, because neither of us could swim, and we'd have sunk below our heads in the mud that the boat was keeping us above. Besides, our guns and other equipment were under water, but still in the boat, and if we left it, we would never find it.

"At first we yelled, hoping some other hunters would come and rescue us. No one did. So finally we took oars and pried our way back to shore. We were froze by the time we got there.

"Both of us went home to get warmed up, but the real kicker came when Smokie went to the Page's store and the owner asked him if he had heard those guys yelling their heads off out on the Lake while everyone else was trying to hunt. Smokie almost brained him."

During the story they located the graves. Duke would now be able to point them out to the gravedigger when the day for transfer came. As Duke walked back to retrieve his grass trimmer and take time for lunch, Fr. Ross got in his car and drove to the rectory. After a sandwich of cold meat and a cup of coffee he headed for his office, which was at the front of the house. Windows on the two outer walls gave him a view of the church and school.

5

Duke Lonergan brought his lumbering Delta 88 to a halt on Oak Street and waited to cross Broadway. Tourists were everywhere, sidewalks were jammed, and cars were lined up waiting to get across the Wisconsin River Bridge. The uptown area was the jumping off spot for the upper Dells boat rides and contained numerous shops and stores. The Strip, as it was called by locals, was on the other side of the river. This five-mile stretch of highway was the site of motels, the lower Dells boat rides, the Ducks, miniature golf courses, and water amusement parks such as Noah's Ark, Family Land, and Riverview, all vying for the tourist dollar.

While amusement park owners tried to keep each tourist in their park with special day-long passes, most felt the urge to see what was on the other side of the river. The bridge across the Wisconsin River tended to be a real bottleneck that tried the patience of any driver whose car was filled with kids impatient to get to the next thrill.

Duke watched the four lanes of traffic surging forward, jockeying for position. He noticed a young man, who seemed out of place in this crowd of tourists, step from the curb. Aimlessly, as if in another world, the man began to cross in front of oncoming traffic.

Horns blared; cars bobbed as drivers jammed on their brakes. Passengers expressed the idiocy of such a move in no uncertain terms. The young man stared at the cars around him, but showed no emotion as he stepped back to the curb. He looked at the "walk/don't walk" signal and then turned to cross in front of Duke's Oldsmobile. He was talking to no one in particular.

"The devil in the box tempted me," he said.

Duke heard but did not understand. He recognized the young man as the one who had been at Mass earlier that morning.

"The devil in the box tempted me," the man said again. "He flashed the green and then changed it when I started to walk. But I must preserve myself and keep myself pure!"

The light changed. The young man stood frozen in position on the sidewalk. Duke glanced in the rear-view mirror as he drove away and noticed that the cluster of people gathered at the light moved slightly away from the man.

"Damn dream," Duke thought to himself as he drove the two blocks down Oak Street toward St. Bridget's.

The dream had returned last night. Once again he had died and once again he found himself in a procession of white-clad, hooded figures making their way toward a brilliant white light. He wasn't afraid. It all seemed so peaceful.

"You have to turn back," his father had told him when they met at the boundary to eternity. Again Duke had walked past him and again his grandparents had given him the message. "You have to return. You have a mission to fulfill."

Only love for his father and grandparents had finally made Duke turn back. As he did, he passed by all those still making their way toward the light. The only face that he could make out was that of Fr. Ross. He did not look at Duke, but kept moving forward. Duke didn't try to call out to his friend. He had a feeling an invisible barrier would have kept him from being heard. Besides, all moved in silence before the light.

"Damn dream," Duke muttered to himself, still debating whether to tell Fr. Ross about it.

6

Krista Elliot worried about Jim. Things had grown worse. He continued to claim that he could see the devil lurking among the flowers printed on the wallpaper in his bedroom. Jim said that he was the Holy One of God. At times, depending on which Bible passage he was reading, he was Abraham sent to start a new people. At other times he was Micah or Zacharia or one of the prophets sent to cleanse the earth.

But always he was God's Holy One. He had been born on July third. Three was a holy number. July was the seventh month of the year, yet another holy number.

"You're crazy," his father, Ed, said, listening to him from his rocker. "You are just crazy."

"I am God's chosen one!" Jim yelled back as he sat by the round kitchen table. "I have been sent to purge this earth with a cleansing fire."

"You've been sent to do shit," responded Ed.

"I am Elijah!"

"The hell you are. Why don't you knock off the bullshit?"

"Who would expect an old drunk to recognize a son of God? You don't deserve any respect. You drank and smoked it all away. Wine bibber!"

Slamming the Bible to the table, Jim jumped from his chair, lifting his arms and screaming at the ceiling. "Send down the fire of Sodom and Gomorrah, Lord! Purify this earth." Ed rocked his way through the outburst in si-

lence, a fire smoldering behind his blue eyes. In an earlier day he would have risen and retaliated, but infir-
mity confined him to his rocking chair. The old man's
only defense against the senselessness of it all was
words.

"Just go. Get out of here and leave your mother and
me alone."

"Young men will see visions and soar like eagles," Jim
declared, still waving his Bible. This scene was played
over and over, every day, and then he would disappear
— up to his bedroom or out to the woods. Sometimes,
he would get into his old red Chevrolet and drive off in
a trail of dust. At times he drove to one of the nearby
towns. At other times he parked along a country road
and sat there, alone.

Through it all Krista worried. She worried about her
son's safety, but more than anything else she worried
about his mind. What had happened while he was gone?
Where had he been? How had he lost that tooth? What
had turned him into a person whom she did not know
and couldn't relate to? Jim had always been her reason
for living. Jim had somehow always secretly understood
that her life was not the easiest, and that their life as a
family was not the best. But Jim had accepted it and
their love for each other had given her the courage to
go on.

Now it was shattered. The boy who brought wildflow-
ers instead of store-bought bouquets, the boy who
bought food for the table instead of something for himself, the boy who shielded his mother from a father's
outbreaks was gone. Hope and the will to live had vanished in a stiff embrace on a summer afternoon.

Krista had her boy back. But how could she restore
the relationship that was her source of survival? She
could endure Ed. Years of poverty had not affected her
spirit. Age itself did not frighten her. What she could
not survive was a son who saw her but did not recognize her, a son who sat at the same table but displayed

no warmth, a son who was no longer a protector but an aggressor.

Krista turned to the only source of help available to her — God. Before Jim had mysteriously left, Krista had always worshipped God as best she could, but she had never asked for anything. When she married Ed, her parents told her that it was not a marriage made in heaven. Ed was a bum, they had stated in no uncertain terms. He was a man with no steady job. He put hunting and fishing ahead of everything else. He was a barroom brawler. A man with no religion. She had been brought up different, they said. But Krista was infatuated by this young man's way with words. Ed had a way of turning each brawl into a prize fight, every fish caught and deer slain into the horn of plenty.

"Don't blame us and don't blame God. You've made your own bed and you will have to sleep in it," her parents had said on the eve of the day before their simple ceremony in a church that made Ed extremely nervous.

As the years went by, Krista neither complained nor blamed. It had been her decision and she accepted it. During her infrequent visits home, which Ed discouraged, she always remained pleasant. If her parents tried to give her anything, she quietly refused. At church she prayed in the manner she had been taught as a child. She followed the prayer book friends had given her during Mass, said her rosary if there was time before Mass, and enjoyed listening to the choir and looking at the stained glass windows. Those were her only contacts with creative beauty. If she spoke to God in a direct fashion, it was always about her son.

She had wanted her son to be handsome and he was. Six feet tall, thin, blue eyes. She had wanted him to be educated. Jim enjoyed books and spent time in the library. Two of the reasons he had joined the Army were to take advantage of its school of electronics and to learn how to fly. Krista had raised him Catholic. Ed refused to go to the baptism. Jim rode to the two weeks of summer religion classes with neighborhood children throughout grade school, made his first communion, and was confirmed in eighth grade. Krista was proud; Ed said nothing. On each occasion she wore the best of her everyday dresses, a bit faded, but clean. When Jim was old enough to drive, he purchased a car with money he had earned and saved. He always took her to Mass on Sunday morning and enjoyed being part of the worship service. At an age when others might have rebelled and refused to go, he did not. Jim seldom dated, preferring to spend his time at home providing for his family, hunting, or working on his Camaro. God had answered her prayers.

But now the work of her prayers had come undone. And as in the past, she knew she must pray, but she also knew that she must take responsibility. Her marriage and her son were the result of her own decisions.

Krista looked up from the row of strawberries to watch Jim drive off. It was obvious that he and Ed had been arguing again. When the pain left her back, she lifted the dishpan of berries she had picked and began to make her way slowly to the house. She was short, five feet three, and had added weight as the years passed. Her legs seemed small beneath her and there was a hitch in her walk.

She opened the gray screen door and made her way to the kitchen sink. She had already washed the strawberries and was clipping the stems off with a paring knife when she spoke to Ed. "Where did Jim go?"

She spoke softly. He was still angry. It wasn't going to be easy.

"Where did Jim go?" She asked just a bit louder. She could hear the rocking chair rock faster and knew Ed heard her.

"Who the hell cares?" Ed growled.

"Ever wonder where he was all that time?"

Silence.

"What do you think happened to him while he was gone?" Silence.

"We've got to do something."

The chair continued to rock. Ed spit in the old Maxwell can. He had given up smoking for chewing.

"Think I'll call the Evans' and see if they will give me a ride into town," Krista said.

She couldn't think of anything else to say or do. She didn't know if Jim would be there or if she would find him, and what she would say if she did, but she had to do something.

The Evans' lived on a farm a short distance away. Elmer and Bernice had often helped Krista, taking her shopping or to the doctor or the pharmacy. Bernice answered on the second ring.

"Bernice, would you help me? I have to talk to Jim and I think he just went to the Dells. I don't know if we can find him."

"What is it, Krista?"

"I don't know. I just don't know. But I have to do something." Krista was on the verge of tears.

"Has he done something to you?"

"No, something is wrong with him. I don't know what it is, but I can't take it any longer. I have to talk to him and find out. He needs help." Tears were flowing freely down Krista's cheeks. She sobbed as she waited for an answer.

"I was putting together a cake," Bernice said. "It can wait. I'll be over and we'll see what we can do. Maybe we can find him." Like many of the neighbors, Bernice knew how important Jim was to Krista and how Krista had waited for his return. She couldn't imagine his return being a source of sorrow.

Krista hung up the phone and walked out on the porch to wait for Bernice. There was no reason to tell Ed that she was doing anything other than going to town to get some groceries. If he knew she was going to look for Jim, it would only anger him. She didn't know what she would do when she found Jim, but she had to begin somewhere. Maybe he could explain what had happened to change him. She would start there.

"He just isn't himself," Krista explained to Bernice as

they passed through Briggsville and drove by the Cove. Jim had always loved fishing in Amey's Pond which lay on the other side of Highway 23. He had hunted ducks there too.

"Something is on his mind, eating away at him," Krista continued. "He's not the person he used to be. I'm his mother and I hardly know him. He's home, but he is a stranger. He argues with Ed. He yells crazy stuff out of the Bible...even claims to see the devil. I don't know. I just don't understand." Tears streamed down Krista's cheeks. The car was filled with an awkward silence.

Traffic increased as they crossed Highway 16 and approached the downtown area. Where to look for Jim? It would be more difficult in the afternoon crowd. Bernice decided to continue across the bridge and go to The Strip. Maybe they could spot his car in a parking lot. God only knew where he could be. He might not even be in town. He had always loved the country. He could have gone anywhere.

Bernice looked in the parking lot just under the railroad overpass. Nothing. But she couldn't really see to the back of the lot. She made a mental note to check it out when they returned and could turn into it without turning across traffic.

The car was not in the lower Dells parking lot or in the Riverview lot. She looked across the street by Deer Park. Again, nothing. They went as far as Fisher's Restaurant. The car was nowhere to be found.

"I wonder," Krista said, as they began to cross the bridge, "if he went to church. He doesn't talk about St. Bridget's, but his mind is filled with the Bible."

They checked the parking lot for the upper Dells boat trips first, then crossed beneath the railroad tracks and up LaCrosse Street. The railroad station was on the right and a feed mill converted into Music Box Gift Shop directly ahead at the intersection with Washington Street. The Old River miniature golf course was on the left. The back of St. Bridget's school came into view as they passed the Gift Shop. A lone car, Jim's Chevrolet, sat in the parking lot. He was somewhere near – if not at church, then perhaps near the public pool or railroad tracks. Bernice pulled into a parking space in front of the church. The overflow tourist crowd had parked almost to the church on Oak Street.

Leaving Bernice in the car, Krista jumped out and, taking one step at a time, climbed to the church's front door. She pulled the glass door open and slipped inside. It was shadowy and cool compared to being outside. The faint smell of burning vigil lights filled the air. After her eyes had adjusted to the dim light, she moved through the inner doors. She could sense the presence of her son.

She finally saw him sitting in the north alcove. His head was bent upward and he seemed to be focusing all of his attention on one of the stained glass windows — that of Elijah.

Jim did not move as his mother walked down the aisle. He had to hear the shuffling of her feet, but his attention was riveted on the window.

"Jim," his mother said reaching out to touch him.

He didn't acknowledge her presence.

"Jim, it is your mother."

"Elijah is moving. He wants to tell me something," Jim said.

"Jim. Please. Let me talk to you." Krista sat in the oak pew beside him grasping one of his hands.

"Elijah...."

"Listen to me, Jim. Who did this to you? What is happening? It is me, your mother. I love you. I love you, Jim. I want you back. I want you to be the person you used to be."

"Elijah...."

"Please. I love you. You're all I've got. Please."

There was a long silence as Krista searched for words. Somehow, she had to talk to her son and get him to talk to her.

Krista rose, continuing to hold her son's hand.

"You need help. We all need help. Come home with

me."

Jim sat for some time and then stood up without saying a word or looking at his mother. She stepped into the aisle and he silently followed. Slowly the gray-haired mother and her tall son left the church.

When they got to Bernice's car Krista let go of his hand and opened the back door on the passenger's side. Jim hesitated as Krista prayed silently. Finally he got in and pulled the door shut. Krista took her place beside Bernice.

"I think we'll go home, Bernice. We have so much to talk about."

Without saying a word Bernice started the car and backed out of the parking space. They turned from Oak Street onto Broadway and were passing the city park between Capital and Bowman when Jim screamed. "You can't capture me. God has set me free!" With that he threw the car door open.

Bernice didn't have a chance to slow down before Jim jumped from the car. He landed on his shoulder and rolled several times and was up and running through the park before they realized what had happened.

Bernice pulled over and they sat in silence as Jim ran down the grassy slope in front of them and across Wisconsin Avenue on the opposite side of the park. He disappeared among the houses between the park and the church.

Bernice broke the silence. "What happened in church?" she asked. Krista was still looking out the window.

"I asked him to come home," she replied.

"What did he say?"

"He talked about Elijah moving in the window and wanting to speak to him. He never really did talk to me, but he seemed willing to come home. I was going to talk to him after we got home."

"Has he acted like this ever since he came home?"

"Ever since."

"You need some help. Something has to be wrong."

"I know, but I just don't know what to do."

"Will you let me help you?"

"Yes."

"Why don't we go to the police? They can help us find him again. Maybe they can help you talk to him."

"Ed won't like it."

"Ed doesn't have to know. Perhaps they can find him quickly and we can talk to him before we go home."

Krista weighed the decision. She didn't want to make Ed mad, and she knew he hated policemen and game wardens. Still, something had to be done. Jim had to have help.

"Krista, let's just try it. They might be able to explain what's happening." Bernice had already started the car and was getting ready to turn and take a side street back to the police station.

Krista said nothing. Bernice turned right again and made her way back to Oak Street. The police station was a nondescript red brick building sandwiched between two others one block from St. Bridget's. Bernice had been a teacher in the Wisconsin Dells public school system before she retired. Maybe it was all the years she had dealt with kids and their problems, but somehow she knew something was wrong. If nothing else, it wouldn't hurt to talk to someone. The first person who came to mind was an acquaintance through school, Dan Iverson. Before inheriting the position as chief of police over a three-man force, Dan had spent time getting to know the community. While summer crowds kept him unusually busy, in the winter he was always available to speak to the students. Winter was also the time when he was more aware of the local citizens' needs. A reported sighting of a stranger in the vicinity of the school would get his immediate attention in the winter. In the summer, strangers were everywhere.

Bernice stopped the car in front of the police station.

"You said that we have to begin somewhere. We tried on our own and it didn't work. I just want you to talk to

Dan Iverson. I've known him for a long time and he won't do anything if you don't want him to. Sometimes it helps to talk to someone who listens." Bernice knew Ed didn't.

They stood on the sidewalk. Krista looked at the two-story, red brick building in front of her. Her childhood training told her it was a place of security. Years of being with Ed made her uncertain.

Bernice held the glass door as Krista entered. Bernice followed her. Wanda Harvey, a former grade school student of Bernice's, was the receptionist. As Krista waited, Bernice approached Wanda who was sorting through a stack of papers lying before her. Wanda looked up and smiled as she recognized Bernice. She remembered her as a caring person.

"Mrs. Evans, what can I do for you?" Wanda asked. Whatever it was, she was going to try to fulfill the wishes of one of her favorite teachers.

"I know it's summer and I hate to bother Dan with something that's probably of little significance, but if he is in, I would like to speak with him," Bernice said. "Mrs. Elliot has been having some problems with her son, Jim, who has come back home after disappearing a few years ago. She doesn't know what is wrong. Neither do I. Dan might be able to help. Krista never has talked to anyone about it." Then Bernice leaned forward and lowered her voice. "I don't know if she will talk now, and I doubt if I can get her to come back if she doesn't." Straightening up, she continued in a conversational tone, "If Dan is present and if he could just take a few moments, I certainly would appreciate it."

Wanda looked beyond Bernice to where Krista was standing. She had never seen Mrs. Elliot before, although she remembered Jim from school. She was struck by her simplicity of dress and her cleanliness. Bernice wasn't the type of person to get carried away. If she sensed something was wrong in this lady's life, there probably was.

"Just a moment while I see if he's in," Wanda replied. She smiled and was gone long enough to express

Bernice's concerns to her boss.

"You can go in. He will be happy to see you, first door on the right," Wanda said when she returned.

The police station had a corridor down its center. Beyond the reception area, the chief of police's office was on the right. A connecting door led to a large conference room, also on the right side of the corridor. Across from the chief's office was a small conference room. There was another office behind it that was shared by those who worked under him. At the end of the corridor was a barred metal door. The Dells police station had six holding cells. Prisoners were kept for only short periods of time in Wisconsin Dells. If their confinement was an extended one, they were taken to the nearby cities of Baraboo or Portage.

Dan Iverson rose as the two ladies entered his office. The oak desk in front of him seemed small, Iverson was a lean six feet four. His dark blue uniform was neatly pressed, thanks to his wife who laid out his uniform each day. His long Scandinavian face bore the lines of time and his once-blond hair was now gray and receding. His blue eyes had paled with time, but they still held a spark that said life is a challenge. Mrs. Iverson always made sure his uniform was fresh and crisply pressed, giving the impression of newness, but one item revealed the length of years he had served – his holster. While his belt was shiny black, his holster, which held a Smith and Wesson .38-caliber revolver, was well worn. Like his gun Dan wanted something that felt comfortable, so, while uniforms and belts and shoes were chosen by his wife, his holster and gun were his to select.

"Good morning, Bernice," Dan greeted her warmly. "How is retirement? I miss you at the school. The bicycle safety courses continue on, you know. I see you have brought a friend."

"Yes, this is Krista Elliot. She's the reason we are visiting," Bernice explained.

Dan walked around his desk and moved one of the

chairs in front of it just slightly, indicating that Bernice should have a seat. Then he placed his hand lightly on Krista's shoulder. "Would you be so kind as to sit here?" He pointed to another chair.

Krista had been absorbing the atmosphere of Dan's office. It seemed friendly and warm. Wood furniture and easy listening music helped, but Dan himself was even more impressive. His hands were large and his touch light. Though his face was hardened by time, his smile was warm. Krista felt welcomed even though she knew Ed would be angry if he knew where she was.

Dan went back to his padded oak swivel chair and sat down. "How can I help two ladies on such a delightful summer day?" he asked.

Bernice spoke first.

"This may be difficult for Krista, but I really think she needs your help or somebody's help. She is not used to talking to anyone and it's going to be hard. Earlier today she called and asked if I would help her look for her son, Jim, who just hasn't been himself. We came to town and found him. We were taking him back to the farm when he jumped from the car and ran away."

Silently Dan turned toward Krista. It had been a number of years since he had seen her and she seemed to have aged a great deal...Portage High School boxing matches...that was it. They had been present whenever their son fought. Those were the only times he had ever seen them but he had heard stories about Ed from his former superior. It was before his time. Ed had been an overnight visitor in one of the back cells more than once. He was rowdy and it was a well-known fact that he poached. The local police and wardens had always looked the other way when it came to Ed's hunting out of season. Ed never took more than the family ate. He was secretive about it and never bragged. It never became a public issue and the authorities were willing to live with it. Besides, Krista and Jim had to eat, and it was an established fact that Krista was not about to beg.

"What's been happening, Krista?"

Krista hesitated.

"I'm here to help you."

"I don't know."

"Give it a try."

Krista looked at him, studying his face.

"Why don't you start at the beginning?"

"It started when Jim came home from the Army and began working in Westfield. I was so proud of him. He was always a good student and had learned how to repair radios in the Army. Well, he worked in Westfield for a while and then got a job in Chicago with a big company. He was so proud when he got that job."

Krista felt more comfortable as she remembered that moment. She, too, had been proud. It seemed that all of her prayers had been answered when Jim sat at their kitchen table and read the letter asking him to report to work.

"At first everything went so well. Jim got an apartment and stayed down there except for weekends when he came home. He talked about his work and showed me his checks. He didn't tell Ed, but he always gave me something. He took out a life insurance policy. He even dated once or twice.

"But then things began to change." Krista's voice grew quieter as she recalled those last days before he had disappeared. "He stopped coming home, and when he did, he didn't talk. He had a red Camaro that he parked under the trees at home and worked on for hours on weekends. It always shined, even the engine. But then he quit cleaning it up. His appearance changed, too. He had bruises, like he had been fighting."

A tear slipped down her cheek as she arrived at the most painful part of her story. "He got to be so distant. He didn't share anything with me. I couldn't talk to him. I knew something was happening, but I couldn't get him to talk about it.

"Then one day he disappeared. I thought he was only going to be gone for a short time, but it got to be days and weeks... three years. I wanted to talk to you, but Ed wouldn't let me. He said Jim would be back, but even at the time that Jim left I was worried.

"Then, the other day, Jim returned. He came driving down the road and parked under the same tree like he had before. I don't know what happened to his Camaro. He was driving a beat-up red and white Chevrolet. The person who got out of that car was my son, but he had changed.

"There is no warmth in his hug. He never talks about himself or where he was. When he does talk, he argues with Ed about the Bible. I brought him up to be a church-goer, but this is different. He sees himself as one of the people in the Bible. The devil is real and moving about in the flowers on the bedroom wallpaper. He uses the Bible to condemn others. Ed thinks he's crazy. I don't know. I just want my son back the way he was before.

"When we went looking for him today, I wanted to talk to him the way we used to talk and find out what is going on. This has to stop. He can't go on like this. When we found him he was at St. Bridget's, sitting, looking at the stained glass window of Elijah and claiming that Elijah was moving and wanting to tell him something. We got him into the car but when we started back, he jumped out while the car was still moving. He said we had captured him and that the gospel had set him free. Something's got to be done."

Krista paused. The chief picked up a ball-point pen and twisted its cap on and off slowly as he tried to sift through the hastily told story. He decided there wasn't an immediate solution. Maybe it would resolve itself; maybe it wouldn't. He would try to meet with Jim and witness first-hand what state of mind the young man was in.

"You never had any trouble with Jim when he was younger?" Dan asked.

"No."

"He never gave you problems when he was in high school?"

"No. He spent a lot of time by himself, but he always helped out at home. We had a big pickle patch and he worked hard caring for it. He was so proud of those checks he brought home."

"He was in the Army?"

"He was at several different bases in the United States during basic training. He was proud of how well he could shoot. It was because he had hunted so much at home and was used to guns. Then he went to Germany. He wrote every other week. He never went off drinking or getting in trouble."

"He changed after he got out of the Army?"

"It seemed like it started when he moved to Chicago. Neighbors noticed it too. When he came home Bernice would see him parked out in the country all by himself, sitting and staring out of the car window. He stopped talking about what was happening in his life."

"And then he left?"

"One day when I was in the garden he said he wouldn't be there to help any more. I thought it was just for the day. But he drove off and didn't come back for three years."

"Has he ever told you where he went?"

"No."

"He never wrote?"

"No. He never called either. I don't know where he was, but it got worse while he was gone."

"He claims to be someone else?"

"He calls himself a messenger from God. Then he goes into all of these numbers and how they prove it."

Dan knew there was no easy solution. He was going to have to find Jim and talk to him. He also knew that he was going to have to gain Krista's confidence and leave Ed out of it for the moment.

"I think the first thing I'll do is look for Jim. Where do you think he went after he jumped from the car?"

"He was headed toward the church. We saw his car parked down behind the school, so I imagine he went there," Bernice said.

"How would it be, Krista, if I talked to Jim? I've got some time so I'll go look for him. In the meantime why don't you go home? After I talk to him I'll call Bernice, and she can either talk to you or bring you in to see me."

Krista's face brightened for the first time in days.

"I came to town hoping something could be done," she said shakily.

"We'll give it a try." Dan rose. He looked impressive to Krista as he rose to full height. A bit gnarled on the outside but with a streak of gentleness inside.

Dan stood behind his desk as Krista followed Bernice to the door.

"Thanks for listening," Bernice said. She paused at the door momentarily, then both women disappeared into the hallway.

7

"**B**e gone for a bit, Wanda," the chief said. "I'm going to look for Jim Elliot. I need to talk to him."

Dan walked out the front door to his blue police car, parked in its reserved spot in front of the station. He had only a rough idea of what Jim looked like. The boy lived in the country and had attended school in Portage. He might have escaped Dan's notice if he had not been part of the school's boxing program. Dan went to the matches from time to time to give out awards. He remembered Jim as an average boxer who tried hard to live up to an image burned into his mind by his father. Dan had felt sorry for Jim.

Where should he start looking? The only clue he had was the old red and white Chevrolet. If he was lucky, Jim was still in town. If not, the search could be put off until another day. It wasn't top priority and Dan was sure that, as the day progressed, something more important would take its place. In the meantime, it wouldn't hurt to be seen patrolling the streets.

Dan was headed east on Broadway when he spotted the car in Field's Big Boy Restaurant's parking lot, noting the Wisconsin license plate as he parked his car. He entered the restaurant through the side door, and acknowledged the smiles of the two high school students who were working behind the counter. Dan got along well with students. He spent many nights at the school during the fall and winter, when there was little else to do. He attended most of the Dells Chiefs football and basketball games.

The crowded booths and tables blocked Dan's view of Jim at first. As he slowly looked through the crowd a second time, he saw Jim sitting alone in a booth near a front window. He was drinking a cup of coffee and reading the Madison State Journal.

Dan studied Jim from a distance, trying to recall what he had looked like as a high school student. His hair was still combed straight back and he wore the same type of clothes – T-shirt with a pocket, blue jeans and running shoes – but he looked different. His face was worn. There was a tooth missing. He seemed preoccupied. As a boxer he had always appeared calm and in control. That was no longer true.

Dan took the long way around the room and came up behind Jim. He had already begun to sit down on the bench across from Jim when he asked permission to do so. Jim glanced up at him and then looked back at his newspaper. He wasn't reading, but was staring at the page intensely, his glazed eyes were glued to the material.

"Devils are hiding behind those buildings," Jim stated without looking up, referring to the pictures illustrating a story on the front page. "If you are divinely inspired, you can see them."

"Jim...remember me? I'm Dan Iverson. I used to come to Portage and watch you box. I remember your match against Dwight Smith. You, the quiet, confident underdog, you outsmarted him and out-pointed him."

Jim looked across the table but did not immediately acknowledge Dan's presence.

"Remember? I helped hand out awards at the banquet. Your mother was so proud. She's a good person," Dan continued.

Jim slowly sipped his coffee.

"I just wanted to be like my father. He always told me he was the greatest fighter of his time. He used to take me to Johnson's Tavern when I was young so I could watch the Wednesday and Friday night fights. I knew all the boxers and their records. I studied all their moves. My father wanted me to be a boxer, but I never lived up to his dreams for me."

"It didn't really matter," Dan said. "Your mother was proud of your grades and the man you were growing up to be. There were better things to do."

"Without the power of God, Paul says we are nothing," Jim said as he pulled the Bible that had been by the window closer to him. "If we have faith the size of a mustard seed, we can move mountains."

"I talked to Krista recently," Dan responded. "She said that you joined the Army after you got out of high school and studied electronics."

"Fort Leonard Wood, Missouri," Jim said, slowly bringing to consciousness a past memory. "Marksman...Sharpshooter...Expert, 69 out of 80 silhouettes. Hit one at 500 meters." Jim then went on to list several more places he had been, "Fort Gordon, Georgia, and Stuttgart, Germany, and Fort McClellan and Fort Rucker, Alabama."

"Hospital." The memory was filled with pain. "They tried to fry my brain. It was just before I left. The doctor said it was part of my medical benefits coming to me as a soldier. Some benefits! They tried to fry my brain. Turn me into a vegetable. Well, nobody is going to do that to me. Not then and not now!" Jim's voice grew louder.

"Jim, where have you been?" Dan asked. "Your mom says that you just up and left one day. She spent a lot of time worrying about you."

Jim didn't answer the question, choosing to introduce a different topic.

"Are you the law?"

"I'm chief of police in Wisconsin Dells."

"Then I want you to go down to Noah's Ark and talk to Bill Beyer. That jackass won't hire me. I'm a veteran. I went down there and picked up trash on my own and put it in the baskets for nothing. But when I asked him for a job, I wasn't good enough. I'm a veteran. Besides, Art Nelson, the lieutenant governor, is a personal friend of mine. I visit his home here in the Dells and I've been at his office many times. If this keeps up. I'm going to call him. Beyer is a jackass. I deserve a job. You're the chief of police; you tell him."

Dan glanced at his watch. He was getting nowhere and was going to have to leave. Jim's conversation baffled him. There was a lot that he didn't know and he must know more if he was to help Krista.

"Have you been going to a doctor?" Dan asked, thinking that if Jim had, he might be able to contact the doctor and get an explanation for Jim's behavior.

"I'm not going to any doctor. The last time they tried to give me Haldol. They forced my mouth open and made me take it. I'm going to sue them. They have no right giving me that medicine. They're trying to destroy my health. First, they fry my brain and try to turn me into a vegetable. Now, they want to destroy me with drugs. They know those drugs are poison. I'm going to tell Lieutenant Governor Nelson what is going on and I am going to sue them."

"I think it might be a wise idea if you got some help."

"My help is in the name of the Lord," Jim answered, picking up his Bible. "If you are an honest chief of police, Dan Iverson, then you will protect me. I need your protection against the evil forces."

"I'll protect you, if you will only listen to me and let me help you. Your mother and I both want to help you."

Jim left without answering. The newspaper was still

lying on the table. A half a cup of cold coffee sat beside it. Dan was looking at both but his eyes weren't focused on either. He really didn't have much to report to Krista. He had found Jim. They had talked. Jim hadn't revealed much, other than that he had perhaps at one time been under treatment for some sort of mental condition. By whom and when, he didn't really know. It was a start. He would have to call some hospitals and see if he could find out which one Jim had been in as a patient. The doctors might be able to give him more information.

The brilliant afternoon sunlight greeted Dan as he walked out of the Big Boy. His thoughts were of Jim but his radio was requesting his presence at one of the local bars.

8

"Kill," said the Voice. "Kill."

"Let me think," Jim cried.

But there was no relief. "Kill," the Voice screamed in his mind, reverberating to the core of his being. "Kill. You are the holy one. You must purify the world of fallen prophets."

Jim knew the Voice. It was a constant companion. At times it roared with so much power it drowned out the radio, no matter how loud it was playing. At other times it spoke in quiet seduction. It had no body. Its domain was the deepest recesses of his brain. At times it was his friend but it was also an enemy, Satan, whom he tried to purge from his system. It was triggered by the figures that he saw darting about in newspaper photographs and from flower to flower in the wallpaper of his bedroom. The Voice had taken complete control of his life.

"You must make a sojourn into the desert," the Voice had commanded as he lay in bed that morning. "You must go back to the land of Skokie and strike at the root of evil."

Jim tried to ignore the Voice at first. Morning was his favorite time. He thought of the fog that hung over Katie's Pond, his favorite childhood fishing spot. It was a backwater of the Big Slough full of smallmouth bass. He had to be careful as he made his way through the cattails to the spot where he had often stood. He could cast a red head all the way across the pond with his spinning rod. With extra effort he could almost reach the end of the pond. Fish were deposited in the pond during the high waters of spring. Few knew about the pond or thought it worth the effort, but Jim had success there.

He thought of another early morning when he had risen before the first light on the opening day of deer season and made his way out into the woods behind the house. Throughout the fall he had watched a buck bed down in those very woods and now, with any luck, it would be his. It was the gray of morning just before the first rays of light broke in the east. The air was crisp, a dusting of snow covered the ground. It was a morning when sound traveled, and he could hear cars in Briggsville which was five miles away. He could hear hunters getting out of their cars at least two miles away. Their hushed voices traveled with clarity. Closing car doors might well have been claps of thunder in the morning stillness. These people thought they were going to sneak up on unsuspecting deer?

Slowly, hoping the wet leaves would muffle his footsteps, he made his way up the hill. There were thick blackberry bushes at the top. In it were numerous deer beds. Jim suspected the buck he was after enjoyed the cover as well as the vantage point.

He remembered the way his nerves had tingled as he approached the edge of the waist-high patch of bushes. He raised his elbows to clear the thorns and snapped off the safety on his bolt action .223 Savage. He took one step on the narrow deer trail leading into the bushes. As he did, he saw the bushes move about twenty yards to his left.

The buck stood to look at him. If it had been later in the nine-day season it would have already been gone. But these were the opening moments of the season; actually it was still twenty minutes before the six-thirty starting time, and not a shot had been fired. Jim raised the rifle and brought the cross hairs to rest behind the buck's shoulder.

It had happened years ago but the memory was vivid. The shot, magnified by the fact that it was too early, rang out and the buck dropped into the thick black-berry bushes.

Jim doubted that a warden would be in the area but he dropped down in the bushes to wait for six-thirty. As if his shot had signaled the unofficial start of the season, he began to hear others. He listened for any sound of movement in the direction of the buck he had just shot, but heard nothing. Finally it was time to claim his prize.

Briars tore at his clothes as he made his way to the spot. He kept his rifle ready in case he had only wounded the deer, but he was certain he had killed it. He had an eight-pointer on opening day.

Jim later cleaned the rack of hair and tissue and mounted it on a homemade plaque. He looked at the antlers now as he rested in bed. He had kept two other sets of antlers during those years, but that early morning hunt and that buck had always been his favorite.

His .223 Savage stood in a homemade cabinet beneath the antlers. There were other guns there including his father's prized Browning automatic shotgun. When it came to bragging with schoolmates about fathers, it was the one thing he could truthfully point out. His father had a Browning automatic, the best there was. His own Remington automatic stood beside it. His dad's lever-action Winchester 30-30 and his pump twenty-two were also there.

It had been a few years since they had been used. Jim could remember how, as a high school student, he had gotten them out and polished them each evening. Before he got his car, they had been his single source of pride. Now they rested in the case behind curtains strung on a rod at the top of the cabinet. He wasn't even sure how many bullets remained in the drawer at the bottom.

"Kill," said the Voice. It slowly overpowered his distracting thoughts.

"Kill. You are the Holy One of God. You were born on the third day of the seventh month. It is the sign of your anointing!"

Struggling to his feet, Jim pulled on his jeans. His mother had washed his clothes and left them stacked on the dresser. He selected fresh socks and a clean T-shirt to wear, then placed some others in a small black traveling bag along with a towel, toothbrush, and razor.

His parents were sleeping when he left the house. Jim quietly closed the screen door and walked across the porch. Dew was still on the grass and he could feel its dampness through his running shoes.

Gravel rattled in the wheel wells of the Chevrolet as he drove out the long driveway. The county roads were deserted at this hour. He took Highway 33 west out of Portage until he reached its intersection with Interstate 90-94, which ran from the northwest part of Wisconsin, past Wisconsin Dells, and on to Milwaukee and Chicago.

Before getting on the I-system he stopped to eat. The restaurant was across from what was now a collection point for an auto auction. Jim remembered it for what it was originally, Olsen's Chevrolet Dealership. The Olsen family was one of the old, established merchants in Portage. When the I-system had cut across the state they saw it as a business opportunity and had opened a garage and showroom at this intersection, hoping to cash in on travelers' car problems. It had worked until car manufacturers fell on hard times. The Olsens sold the business before it failed.

Jim remembered buying his Camaro there. He remembered the salesman and the three-year loan he had agreed to. He hadn't worried about paying it. He was single and living with his parents. He had a job at the Portage Creamery and the promise of an even better job in Chicago. He was sure of steady employment.

The 350 engine had surged with power as he drove it home. It was one of the proudest moments of his life, one that he first shared with his mother. He had taken her on a long ride that day through Wisconsin Dells and Portage. He remembered how happy she was.

But that was before Chicago. Now the Voice was directing him to return to where it had all begun. He looked up from his table and stared at the television set that was on a shelf high enough for all customers to see. "Headline News" was on, but it was not the news that Jim saw.

"Kill." The Voice now had a form that he could see in the screen. A prophet's face twisted in anger. An arm raised high, its bony finger admonishing him.

"You must go back to Skokie and kill the false prophet who could not save you from the devil. You must kill the priest who could give you no release in his confessional!"

Jim glanced away from the television screen. As he looked out the window, another scene appeared. This time the window served as entrance into the pits of hell. Flames reached everywhere. Smoke billowed forth. Figures darted about. A devil's voice taunted him. "These false prophets can bring no release. You are the prophet. You alone do I fear, but you must gain your release in order to gain power."

Jim paid his bill and walked out into the fresh summer air. As he drove onto the interstate he could see the vacant Cascade Ski Resort. Its runs were grass-covered, the lifts silent. The tourists who were streaming up the highway were traveling another fifteen minutes north to Wisconsin Dells.

When Jim reached Madison he stopped again for coffee at the Union 76 truck stop. He left a half-full cup on the table in the booth. The Voice was prodding him to move on. He started his car, circled around behind the restaurant, and made his way to the traffic light on Business Highway 51. Soon he was back on the interstate, heading east. At the intersection he turned toward Milwaukee.

He stopped at the McDonald's on Moorland Drive for another cup of coffee, drove to a nearby gas station, and was again on his way. He took the I-894 bypass around Milwaukee, and then took I-94 south toward Chicago. From the Edens Expressway Jim exited on Dempster Avenue and drove toward St. Peter's Church and rectory at the intersection of Lincoln Avenue and Niles Center Road. Directly across the street were the cemetery and funeral home. The three were so close together that a hearse was unnecessary. Pallbearers carried the casket across the street for the funeral ceremony, and then back across the street to the cemetery.

Jim found a parking place near the old fire station, which now served as headquarters for the Skokie Historical Society. In the dark of night he could make an easy escape from the back of the cemetery to his car.

He walked to the Village Pub on the corner. The table at the front window wasn't the best place for viewing the church but he could see the street that separated the church and cemetery. With any luck he would catch a glimpse of Fr. Shane McLaughlin.

Fr. McLaughlin had served at St. Peter's for thirty years before his retirement. The Chicago Diocese had been kind enough to let him live in the rectory as pastor emeritus after his retirement. He still took the 6:30 a.m. Mass, if for no other reason than he was always awake at that hour and the other two priests weren't. He also led a rosary at 5:30 p.m. and occasionally presided at a wake or celebrated a funeral if asked to do so. Whenever a funeral was held Fr. McLaughlin could be found in the back pew. St. Peter's congregation was his family. They had grown old together.

The remnants of a once vital, but now aging, Holy Name Society gathered once a month to play cards in the church basement. It was among these men that Fr. McLaughlin felt most at ease. Like him, most of the men who gathered were retired. Many could remember when the city was little more than open fields.

Those days were memories to be shared over a round of sheepshead. While the church had served as the spiritual headquarters for the area, the many bars in the area had served as the social headquarters. The C&W Tap was typical. Bottles of liquor lined the back bar but bartender Michael Baumhardt always greeted his patrons with the question, "Shot or beer?" If the response was for anything different he was quick to respond, "This isn't a social club."

During the Prohibition, Albert Alf's Bar and Hall, located on Niles Center Road near St. Peter's, became a soft drink parlor, at least on the surface. Al Capone's men were ever present to take orders.

At one point a friend of Albert's, Herman Schiller, decided he was going to build a brewery in his barn. To ensure the quality he hired a foreign braumeister. On the day the brewery was completed, Al Capone, under the pretext of wishing them well, held a grand opening party at Vossnow's Restaurant. At the appropriate time he got up to toast them: "I'm glad you could show up, you Dutch bastards. I just want you to know you have made your last barrel of beer." As Schiller and his friends left the restaurant they could see smoke rising on the horizon from their burning barn. Their operation lasted exactly one day.

The day before New Year's was a favorite time to raid speakeasies because federal agents knew they would be stocked for the holiday. As the story was told, on one occasion those arrested in Skokie were taken to the jail in Wheeling, a city in nearby Lake County. On New Year's Day a truck appeared at the jail with all the supplies needed for a party. A second truck brought the band and broads. If those arrested couldn't be at the party, Big Al would bring the party to them.

As the night wore on and stories were exchanged, the

tale of Gustaf Wenzel emerged. Wenzel, nicknamed Squeegee because he was so tight with his money, was challenged by the patrons at Albert's to chug a schooner, or 32 ounces of beer. Gustaf thought about it, then walked next door to Duffy's Tavern to give it a try. When the experiment proved successful, he went back to Albert's and accepted the bet.

There was the pool hall where one played for a penny a minute. The Niles Center Recreation Hall, owned by Albert Lies, offered both bowling and pool. It was there that young men like Ed Alf and Rudy Heinze were willing to hustle you. According to the men who gathered at St. Peter's, you could still see bullet holes in the walls that remained from the days of a gangland shoot out.

Fr. McLaughlin could relate to those days. He had his own stories of the Holy Name Society gathering for the eight o'clock Mass and then eating breakfast in the church basement after Mass. He could also recall the closing of forty hours devotions and how many of these same men, as Knights of Columbus, had stood with their swords forming an arch under which the gathering of priests marched on their way up the center aisle.

They were memories from a different era. The last of the card players who had met in the church basement was gone now. Fr McLaughlin picked up the last of the beer cans and put the partially emptied bottle of Kessler's in the refrigerator in the kitchen. He made sure all the tables and chairs were in place, walked to a side door and glanced back before opening the door and turning off the lights.

Crisp midnight air greeted him as he locked the door and glanced down the street. The rectory, which was directly behind the church, was dark. His fellow priests were asleep. Light fog partially obscured the streetlights.

"Care to take a walk?" the voice from the shadows asked Fr. McLaughlin.

It startled the old priest. He took an unsure step and turned, just as a strong arm wrapped itself below his chest and squeezed hard. He couldn't make a sound. The air had been forced from his lungs.

As the pressure eased, Fr. McLaughlin gasped. He noticed an odor that he associated with hospitals. Then he passed out.

Consciousness brought more darkness, a darkness filled with the dampness of night. He tried to wipe his eyes but felt the bite of a chain against his wrists. His legs were also chained. He was lying on his back. He tried to move but felt sharp stabbing pain in his legs and back.

He looked up through the darkness and saw three white figures. He recognized a face looking down at him. It was the face of Christ looking down from a crucifix. Fr. McLaughlin was chained to the altar in the cemetery.

"The Beast has been chained," whispered a voice close to Fr. McLaughlin's ear.

Fr. McLaughlin struggled to turn his head toward his persecutor, but a strong hand clamped to his throat prevented him from doing so.

The hand tore the duct tape from his mouth, then returned to his throat.

"Don't try to scream," said the voice. "If you do, I will crush your throat."

Silence followed. Fr. McLaughlin felt the warmth of blood on his forehead. He struggled to understand. Who was this attacker? What did he want? Why the cemetery? Even if he wanted to resist, his thin frail body was no match for the aggressor.

"Feel that blood on your forehead, Father?" the voice asked. "I have marked you with the sign of the Beast for that is what you are! You are a false prophet who has led the flock astray."

Fr. McLaughlin twisted his head as much as the vise grip of the hand on his throat would permit and whispered through twisted lips, "Who are you?"

"Don't you remember me, Father? You should remember me. I lived in your parish. I was working in a factory. Spirits began to take over my life and I came to you in confession. I pleaded with you to drive them out of me. The forces of good and evil were fighting within me. I asked you to cast Satan from me. You didn't do it, Father, and the people at work laughed at me. I was Christ, and like Christ, those at work beat me. See this missing tooth?" The figure beside Fr. McLaughlin leaned toward him for a moment and pressed the index finger of his free hand to a gap in his mouth. "They beat me like they beat Christ. Guards hauled me away."

"Remember?" Fr. McLaughlin's captor whispered harshly.

"I remember nothing," Fr. McLaughlin whispered. "If I caused you to be hurt, I am sorry."

"The soothing words of the devil," the voice replied. "But I, the third angel of the Apocalypse, have exposed you. Now it is time for you to drink the wine of God's anger. The scriptures say that you shall be tormented with fire and burning sulfur in the presence of the holy angels and the Lamb. The smoke of your torture shall rise forever and there will be no relief day or night, for you have worshipped the Creature and have been tattooed with the code of his name.

"It is all in the scriptures and now the Lamb looks down upon you, waiting for you to be destroyed in smoke and sulfur." The hand that had grasped his throat was gone but the pain remained. Fr. McLaughlin struggled to get words from his throat. None came. If he could speak he wouldn't know what to say.

Fr. McLaughlin watched as the figure twisted the cap off an old red metal gas can. The smell of the liquid filled his nostrils. It felt cold as it soaked through his clothes. Then he watched the figure pour the rest of the gas around the base of the altar and fling the can into the darkness of the cemetery.

"Fire and sulfur, Father! Fire and sulfur."

There was a white spark, then the head of the wooden match burst into flame.

"God, have mercy on my soul," the priest whispered.

"It is too late for mercy. You should have thought before you sold your soul to the Devil!"

The Voice tore through Jim's brain, echoed through his very being. "Kill!" For a moment his whole being froze in the darkness. Then he raised his arm. The cemetery shook beneath him as he plunged his arm forward. The Voice thundered, "Kill!"

"I am the new Elijah!" Jim shouted. "I have come to destroy the false prophets upon an altar."

The flames spread slowly at first. Then in one quick burst they consumed the altar and leapt toward the heavens, enveloping Fr. McLaughlin's body. As Jim ran through the cemetery he looked back and saw the face of Christ illumined by the flames, white against the darkness of the night. He waited for the scream which would be a sign that the new Elijah had triumphed.

9

Duke hated dusting. Dusting wasn't manly. He skipped it when he could, but he knew that if he skipped it on this weekend, it would be noticeable. He left it for last. He had replaced all of the burned out candles in the outdoor shrine. He had mowed the grass and used the weed-eater to make sure everything looked its best for the Saturday afternoon crowd. There was nothing left to do but get the inside of the church ready. He still hated it. His thick, callused hands just weren't made for a dust cloth.

Duke was giving the railing on the choir loft a very light once-over when he noticed Fr. Ross walking through the sacristy door. It was mid-afternoon and he suspected that Fr. Ross was deep into sermon preparation. As Fr. Ross walked to the lectern that had been fashioned from the old communion railing, and opened the book of readings, he surmised that his first observation had been a correct one.

Duke studied Fr. Ross from above. For a man who ate most of his meals on the run either in his car or at his desk he looked tremendously fit. Duke was always amazed on those occasions when at noon he would be sitting in Fr. Ross' office reporting on his yard work and it came time to eat. A salad, fruit, a piece of bread and a cup of coffee was the standard meal. Preparations usually began at noon and, with phone calls and visits, the actual eating usually took place between two and three o'clock.

Duke guessed his height at five-eight. He always looked tan. From his position in the choir loft, the priest's baldness was quite evident. Fr. Ross didn't do anything to hide it. He combed the dark black hair on the sides of his head straight back. The wisps of hair that remained on top got the same treatment. Habit caused him to pull his comb from a pocket and run it through his hair.

While many priests had changed to other colors in the post-Vatican era, Fr. Ross preferred black. His shoes and slacks were always black, as were his suits. While parishioners and friends often gave him colorful sport shirts, he preferred to wear black or white. Neatness was more important to him than color.

Fr. Ross needed glasses for reading. He used drug store glasses even though he had brown plastic-framed prescription ones. Glancing over his glasses as he studied the open lectionary, he saw Duke looking down at him.

"Is that a new saint's statue I see in the choir loft?"

"Never saw a saint dressed in bib overalls."

"St. Isadore was. I see you're at your favorite task, Duke."

"Not really."

"Did you dust down here last week?"

"Lightly."

"Awful light!"

"I'm on my way."

"Um hum." Fr. Ross knew he was never going to get Duke to change his attitude. There was no use pushing the issue.

"I noticed you edged the sidewalk in front of the school. It looks good."

Duke appreciated the change of topic.

"Got it done yesterday afternoon. I'm going to do the church side on Monday."

Fr. Ross looked back down at the lectionary. There was a period of silence. Duke had moved from the choir loft to the sanctuary.

"Have you noticed a stranger hanging around church lately?"

Duke asked.

"Stranger?"

"Young man. Wears Levi's and a colored T-shirt most of the time. Drives an old red and white Chevrolet."

"Yes. In fact, I think I talked to him one day when I was coming across the street. Why?"

"I don't know. He just gives me the creeps."

"He comes into church often during the day. Sits in front of that window with Elijah in it. Talks to it. Makes me edgy."

Why did the name Elijah mean something to him? The strange confession, Fr. Ross thought to himself, but said nothing.

"I have seen him at Mass. I don't know who he is though."

"His name is Jim Elliot. He and his parents live on a farm outside of town."

Duke had asked Dan Iverson one day when the police chief was making his rounds through the cemetery. "His mother comes to church on Sundays with the neighbors. Real poor. Jim was gone for a while. Just disappeared for three years." Duke volunteered another piece of information he had received from Dan. "No one knows where he was."

"I wasn't aware of that."

"Strangest thing. I was at a stoplight the other day and there he was. Stepped right out in front of traffic and almost got run over. When it was over, he said it was the devil playing tricks on him by changing the lights when he got halfway across."

"I think the devil has more to do than change traffic lights in downtown Wisconsin Dells."

"Not if you talked to this guy."

"Thanks for telling me, Duke. I appreciate it. In the meantime if you see him around here, keep an eye on him."

Duke nodded. Keeping an eye on him sanctioned him to watch and listen from the choir loft.

Perhaps he was just one of those visionaries who seemed to pass through the Dells in the summer, Fr. Ross thought to himself as he walked from the church to the garage. It was still early Saturday afternoon and his conscience had been bothering him for two days. Thelma Dewsnap had been admitted to St. Clare's Hospital in Baraboo and he hadn't had the opportunity to visit her.

Maybe he just found it hard. Thelma had been diagnosed with bone cancer. She had stayed at home as long as she could. He had visited her every Friday since she received the news. He knew from past cases the pain she would go through. She would not get better, from now on, with each visit, she would waste away before his eyes.

She had asked one Friday, with the simplicity of a saint, why there was so much pain. "I must have done something terribly wrong when I was young," she said.

"I doubt that very much," Fr. Ross responded. He was at a loss for words. "I think you are and will be a great saint." A great one indeed. He thought of the suffering that she had gone through and would go through. If he never had to visit another cancer patient it would be a happy day.

When he preached on the subject he often talked about how man, not God, lets such things exist. "It would be interesting if we, as a country, had put as much money into the research of remedies for certain diseases as we have war materials. Cancer might be a dis-

ease of the past," he said. And then he would finish
with the comment, "Can you imagine if we funded our
wars by placing canisters on drug store counters and
used tax money to find a cure for cancer? Research
might have eliminated that disease." It wasn't that he
was opposed to bearing arms so much as he was tired
of walking through hospital doors. Yet he knew it would
never stop. Sickness was a part of the human condition. It had been a preoccupation of Christ's.

Fr. Ross took Highway A, the back road to Baraboo.
One of the amphibious ducks, WWII vehicles capable
of traveling on land and water, was just coming out of
Lake Delton. No doubt the tourists sitting in the back
had gotten wet as the boat plunged into the lake. Slow
or fast, the driver always asked. The riders always
chose to go in fast creating a large wave that rolled back
into the stern of the duck.

While on the lake the driver would encourage everyone to look out the back of the boat, and then tell them
they could go home and tell people they had had the
unique experience of looking out a duck's ass.

Further along on the tour the driver would point to
three overhead steel beams and tell his audience that
it was a training ground for duck drivers. They were to
put three marbles in their mouth and spit one out each
time they had successfully walked across the gorge on
a beam. When they lost all their marbles they were
qualified to be a duck driver.

Fr. Ross knew all the stories well enough to be a guide
himself. When friends came to visit, one of the favorite
rides was a tour of the Wisconsin River and surrounding area on the Wisconsin Dells Ducks. Fr. Ross forgot
the number of times he had taken the tour but often,
under his breath, he gave the memorized tour along
with the guide.

10

By the time Fr. Ross returned from visiting Thelma Dewsnap at the Baraboo Hospital, Leroy Phillips was standing by the front door of the church, waiting for the door to be unlocked. Leroy was retired. He lived three houses away from the church. If he was in town on Saturday and not visiting his son in Milwaukee, where he had lived before retiring, he made it a point of arriving fifteen minutes before confessions so he could get his spot on the inside aisle in the very last pew on the left. If Fr. Ross was inside preparing and had forgotten to unlock the doors, Leroy reminded him by banging his cane on the metal frame of the glass doors. He was impatiently banging on the doors now.

Fr. Ross openly joked with those who considered spots in the back pews their very own. He compared it to the earlier days of farming when each cow had its own stanchion. If a cow came into the barn and found another cow in its spot, it walked back and forth in the aisle, stubbornly waiting for the cow to leave. If it didn't, the impatient late-arrival would finally plunge in between the two standing cows and put its head right in the stanchion with the cow already there. "You'd do the same," he joked, "if someone sat in your spot!"

One weekday morning he was surprised when Mildred Wade came walking out of church before Mass got under way. "Someone took my place," declared Mildred as she made her way to her car and drove off.

Now as Fr. Ross hastened along the sidewalk to the side door of the rectory, he recalled still another occasion in which he had almost been late for weekday Mass. Duke had invited him over to Endeavor for an early morning breakfast at the Chicken Inn. The purpose had not been so much to have breakfast as to tell Fr. Ross about a friend in a Michigan hospital who was dying of cancer.

"Would you please call him?" Duke had asked. "You will know what to say."

They had talked so long and intently that Fr. Ross hadn't paid attention to the time and had to race back to the Dells for the morning Mass. As he ran in one side of the rectory and out the other he was greeted by a student selling pizza for a school fund-raiser. "No time," Fr. Ross said to the boy who had been patiently waiting. "I've only got three minutes before Mass starts."

He put off calling Duke's friend until afternoon, searching for what to say. Eventually Fr. Ross made the call. The next day the man died.

Fr. Ross remembered still another occasion when he had been asked to visit a total stranger in St. Mary's burn center in Milwaukee. The man had fallen into an electric generator in a paper mill in Port Edwards. The only spot on his body that wasn't burned was where his belt buckle had been. "He is Lutheran," the person making the request had stated. "But he will understand." Fr. Ross had gotten up early and made the four-hour round trip to Milwaukee before the morning Mass. Later he found out he was the last person to speak with the man. By breakfast time the man slipped into a coma. A day later he was dead.

Now Fr. Ross once again found himself rushing through the rectory, grabbing his sermon materials from the table beside his recliner and his personal chalice from its place in the office. He ran out the side door and headed toward the church.

He quickly set the chalice and folder on the vesting counter in the church and walked down the center aisle to open the door for Leroy, who continued to bang impatiently with his cane.

"Leroy, get in here," Fr. Ross said in a loud voice to make sure that Leroy, who wore two hearing aids, heard him. "You are going to sunburn the top of your head." Leroy had a broad, flat bald head with a fringe of gray hair. He walked with a stoop and a slow shuffle. His silver-framed glasses remained in his pocket until he was seated. Leroy couldn't wear them when he walked for fear they would fall off, because his bent back caused his face to be pitched so far forward and down.

Leroy's first words to Fr. Ross were usually in the form of a question. His most recent concern was a neighboring church that removed their kneelers. It didn't seem to matter that he no longer was able to kneel at Mass.

Tonight his comment was of a different nature. "Took a nap and overslept?" he asked.

Fr. Ross had learned never to try and explain things. People already had a mindset from which they worked. In this case it was not a matter of forgetting to open the doors before going to the hospital or that Fr. Ross had been on a mission of mercy. Priests had a life of ease in Leroy's mind.

"Isn't an afternoon nap on a Saturday delightful?" Fr. Ross asked in return.

Leroy raised a crooked finger and asked a question about last week's bulletin having the wrong date on it. "Just a printer's mistake," Fr. Ross explained as he turned to make his way up the center aisle and prepare for Mass. He had only five minutes to turn the books to the proper pages, prepare his chalice, take the ciboriums to the back of church, and open the windows.

Five minutes had already gone by in the period assigned for confessions as Fr. Ross walked down the aisle with the ciboriums and his sermon material in hand. Leroy Phillips remained the only person in church. Fr. Ross set the ciboriums on the little table behind Phillips and, after an exchange of comments with Leroy, took his place in the confessional.

Ten more minutes went by before the door opened and someone entered and knelt down. Fr. Ross closed the leather folder that contained his sermon notes and slid open the small wooden door that separated him from the penitent.

"Bless me, Father, for I have sinned. My last confession was about a week ago. I accuse myself of the following sins. But before I make my confession I must ask if you are a true priest of God."

The voice on the other side of the screen went silent. It was faint but Fr. Ross recognized it as a male voice. The request was a strange one. One would presume that if a priest were in a confessional in a Catholic Church that priest would have the necessary faculties to hear confession.

"Yes," Fr. Ross replied. "I am an ordained priest in the Madison Diocese. I have been for over 30 years."

"But are you a true priest of God?"

"As true as they come."

"I need a true priest of God to lift the burden from my soul. There are so many false priests. They have tried to lift the burden, and like the false priests of Baal have failed. I am searching for a true priest who can lift the veil from my eyes."

"I am a validly ordained priest. All I can do is try." Fr. Ross began to wonder where this conversation was taking him. There was something about the voice and the content of the confession that seemed familiar, but he had learned never to try and guess who was on the other side of that screen.

"I need a true priest of God who knows good and evil. There are many voices crying out in my mind and I need a true priest who, like Elijah, can destroy the wicked ones. I want to be a true servant of God. I want God's voice to direct me.

"I have met priests who said they were true priests only to find out they have been false ones," the penitent continued. "Later the voice of God has told me so and sent me back to destroy them.

"I am a messenger of God. I was born on July third. July is the seventh month of the year. I am a holy one of God.

"If you are a true priest you can forgive my sins. You can lift the veil."

Fr. Ross guessed that it was the person who had been

to confession, but walked out in a rage.

"I'm confused," the voice continued. "The voice behind the flowers. I heard it. It told me to kill. But it turned out to be Lucifer, not God. The Prince of Devils. He tricked me."

The voice on the other side of the screen became silent. Fr. Ross was certain of the voice now. Without revealing that he knew the person had been there before he began to encourage him to seek out a priest for a further discussion.

"Would it be possible to come in during the week or find another priest to talk to?" Fr. Ross asked. "I just feel this is a matter that will take some time." He was also beginning to feel that this was a matter that was beyond his expertise. Fr. Ross was beginning to question the person's mental competence. "I will be here all week. You could make an appointment. There are other priests in Portage...Reedsburg...Baraboo. Any of us would be willing to help you."

"I am a holy one of God," the penitent said. "I have set ablaze the fire on the altar, and it has consumed everything on it! You must be a true priest if I am to talk to you."

"You really should talk to someone," Fr. Ross said, wondering if he was making any impression at all.

The voice became silent, and then the silence was interrupted by the opening of the door on the opposite side of Fr. Ross. A cane bumped against the wall of the confessional and the next penitent knelt heavily on the kneeler.

"I am the holy one of God. The voice has told me to kill...," said a barely audible voice. Fr. Ross heard the person rise to leave. The door opened and there was a moment of silence before Fr. Ross slid the small door closed and opened the one on the opposite side. The lady behind the screen spoke so softly that Fr. Ross could not hear her. But he did not ask her to speak up. His thoughts were on the previous penitent.

A martyr's death was something Fr. Ross thought of

from time to time. It seemed that many times the people who were remembered after death were those who had died young and tragically. But he wondered if he would have the courage it took to be that kind of person. He remembered a meditation he did in which the lesson was that the most difficult moment in decision-making was the moment before the plan was to go into operation. Once a person got involved in the execution of a decision, the panic disappeared.

The writer had used parachuting from a plane as an example. A person's blood pressure is considerably higher right before the jump than after the jump. Fr. Ross compared that to his own facing of a martyr's death. The decision to undergo it would be difficult. The moments before the executioner began to act would be filled with anxiety and second thoughts. But once the torture had begun?

Fr. Ross was jarred back into the present by a rustle on the other side of the screen. It signaled the person had finished. He gave a penance and told the person to go in peace. It was a peace he could not share.

Duke Lonergan made his customary appearance at Fr. Ross' side on the front steps within seconds of Fr. Ross' getting there. As Duke reviewed what he had done the day before, he caught sight of Rose Wells coming up the steps. He stopped in the middle of the sentence.

Rose had gone through three husbands and was in search of a fourth. She was going on sixty and dressed like she was approaching thirty, ready for a night on the town rather than church. Tonight she wore black high heels, black stockings with a bold pattern, and a leather mini-skirt. Her white knit top outlined her well-endowed upper body. Duke suspected she used a bra that accentuated her ample cleavage. It would be hard for the old men in the back of the church where she sat to concentrate on their prayers tonight. Some would probably get a sharp elbow from their wives.

Rose stood in front of Fr. Ross. She had once confided that she thought she was destined to have a place in his life. He had assured her she wasn't.

"*F..a..thur?*" Rose always dragged out the first part of the word and turned it into a question. Her make-up had been liberally applied and looked oily. She wore large-rimmed plastic glasses. The lens did not hide her bold use of eyeliner, eye shadow, and mascara. On this evening her hair was dyed black to match her apparel.

"*F..a..thur?*" Rose repeated as if she didn't have his full attention. "Can I make an appointment to see you?"

"What would you like to see me about?" asked Fr. Ross. He really wanted to know if it was for the sake of a visit or if she really had something to discuss. He tried to limit his contact with her to phone conversations, and if there was a need for her to come to the rectory, it was only when a secretary or someone else was in the house. The last thing he wanted was her making some unfounded accusation against him.

"The people I work with at the hotel have been talking about you, and I can't believe what they said." Rose worked as a maid at the River Inn.

"Why don't you call me later tonight and tell me?" Fr. Ross said. "I don't think you have to come to see me in order to tell me."

"*F..a..thur?*"

"Call me," Fr. Ross repeated.

As Rose went into church, Duke turned to Fr. Ross with a smile. "You should see her when she mows her lawn. She wears a leopard-skin bikini. If you don't think that hasn't changed the driving patterns of the retired men in town!" He didn't add that sometimes it changed his own way of going from the church to the cemetery.

Duke's serious expression changed to a subtle smile as he asked in a voice low enough to keep those entering church from hearing, "Do you think she can see her shoes?"

Duke knew Fr. Ross would never answer that question, so he asked another, "What do you think when you see someone like that?"

"I don't think," Fr. Ross said as he turned his attention to others who were coming in. Duke decided it was time for him to walk back down the steps and check the vigil lights in the Blessed Mother Shrine. This would give him an opportunity to get rid of his cigarette. He knew if he stubbed it out and dropped it over the wall onto the lawn, Fr. Ross would have something to say to him.

Later that evening Rose called.

"*F..a..thur?*"

"Yes, Rose."

"*F..a..thur,* do you know what they have been saying about you in the lunch room at the River Inn?"

"No. I'm afraid I don't."

"They say that you go up to Leo's in Lyndon Station and get fall-down drunk every night. Is that true?"

"Rose. Let me just say this. I have only been in Lyndon Station twice. One time I had a funeral for a young boy who died in an accident. The parents knew me and wanted me to have the funeral. Another time I drove through on the way to a burial in a cemetery on the other side of the town.

"Another thing. I don't drink. How could I possibly be in Lyndon Station getting drunk every night?"

"But *F..a..thur,* why would this lady say this if it wasn't true?"

"Rose. I have no idea, and I really don't care. I am not a saint but I try to live the best life I can. I have no control over what other people say. Because I don't drink I find it amusing."

"But...why would she say it?"

"I don't know. Maybe you should ask her. Thank you for calling."

"*F..a..thur?*"

"Good night, Rose."

Fr. Ross turned back to his newspaper. He had given up drinking several years ago just so he wouldn't have to deal with such accusations. If he went to a restaurant and had a drink before dinner and another after, someone was bound to accuse him of being a drunk.

This way he had a definite comeback to any such accusations.

Fr. Ross always looked at the Life section of USA Today first, because he often found sermon materials in that section. Then he turned to the Sports and Money sections and finally the main news section. It was late by the time he got to the news section on this particular Saturday night. He skimmed it before going upstairs to bed.

Had he looked at the Nationline column, he might have found some interest in a paragraph entitled, "Priest Slain." The article described how a retired priest, Fr. Shane McLaughlin, had been brutally murdered in the Chicago suburb of Skokie. Firemen had been called to the cemetery at St. Peter's Parish only to discover his body amid the flames on an altar in the cemetery.

11

A lex Williams had been at daily Mass. His comments before and after Mass always got Fr. Ross' day off to a good start. Alex was retired and usually interrupted his early morning cribbage game, unless the money was too inviting, to come to the 8 o'clock Mass. He frequently joked about the days when he drank heavily. "I really wasn't crawling home. I was teaching my dog to retrieve."

Alex drew the "tsk, tsk," of the predominantly gray-haired female audience with remarks about a fictitious feud with his wife. He publicly announced, "Father, you have to be quick. My wife and I are in a good argument. If I don't get home quick, we'll forget where we are and have to start over.

"When my wife tells me we are having a roast for supper, I get up and run," he said on another occasion.

This morning the subject of conversation had been fishing. Fr. Ross asked him if he had ever gone fishing for salmon in Lake Michigan.

"No way," Alex had replied. "The last time they asked me to get on a boat I ended up in the Philippines and Japan. They told me we were going fishing that time, too."

Fr. Ross needed those comments, especially on this day, to get him through his weekly communion calls. He was about to spend his morning visiting the sick and shut-ins, a journey he often referred to as a "bath in depression."

Fr. Ross hated spending money on automobiles. His old, beat-up vehicle eliminated complaints about priests always having new cars. Then, as he often told Duke when Duke told him he deserved a better vehicle, "What if I appeared for the last judgment and Jesus arrived in a rusty 1977 Chevrolet Caprice and I arrived in a $46,000 Lincoln Town Car?" Duke finally conceded, "You may have something. He did ride a donkey the first time around."

Fr. Ross' practice of buying old vehicles for cash had started with his purchase of a telephone van for $2,000 which he drove 100,000 miles. He had fond memories of that van. It was little more than a motor, transmission, and rear end. It had no radio. The heater didn't have a chance of overcoming the cold that came in through two large holes behind the rear wheels. The clutch linkage fell apart, leaving Fr. Ross stranded in high gear. The headlights went out when switching from high to low beam.

But the van had its advantages. Panhandlers failed to recognize it as a vehicle a priest might drive. On one occasion, while dressed for yard work outside the rectory, a panhandler approached him and asked if the priest was at home. Fr. Ross quickly took advantage of not being recognized as a priest.

"I don't think so," he said. "Even if he was, he wouldn't give you anything. He's tough as nails. But I'll tell you what. I know a church where they are pretty free with handouts. Jump in my van."

Fr. Ross reached across the seat and opened the passenger door. The panhandler jumped in. They were soon on a cross town journey. Fr. Ross stopped in front of the Lutheran parsonage, pointed to the door, and sent the man on his way. Then he drove off, hoping the Lutheran pastor hadn't seen him.

More than once the van had become part of his sermon. A friend who had come to Fr. Ross' first weekend Mass in Wisconsin Dells loved repeating its role in his first sermon. "I was in one of the back pews and there were three elderly ladies sitting in front of me, sizing up their new pastor. They were all nodding in approval until he got to the part about his van, which was in its last weeks of existence.

"Then Fr. Ross starts talking about his van. 'If anybody steals that van, I'll kill 'em!' Fr. Ross shouted. The gray-haired ladies were aghast! After a pause Fr. Ross added, 'If they bring it back.'"

The blue van came to an ignominious end after a sympathetic dealer took it off Fr. Ross' hands in trade for a used Ford Ranger. The person who bought the van thought it looked inconspicuous enough to use for hauling illegal gambling devices. The police eventually arrested him and confiscated the van.

The Ford Ranger went 364,000 miles before colliding with a pig in the middle of the night on a return trip from Mayo Clinic in Rochester, Minnesota. The insurance agent had laughed when Fr. Ross called. "This time consider it totaled," he advised before Fr. Ross had an opportunity to argue for its repair.

Fr. Ross backed the Ranger's replacement, a 1984 Fiero, out of the garage. Although the odometer didn't work, the previous owner assured him the car had only 68,000 miles on it. No, it didn't have floor mats. They had been ruined in a flood. The flood had also destroyed the wiring system but most of that had been repaired. Paint had chipped off the hood and the passenger side was damaged. It could be fixed for $200. The motor that raised the window on the passenger side also didn't work. It wouldn't take much to restore everything according to the owner, who wanted $1,000 for it.

Fr. Ross offered $500 and got it. Eight months later it still had not been repaired. As Fr. Ross backed it out of the garage, he knew one repair that had to be made. The flood had destroyed the wiring that controlled the heater. Fr. Ross hadn't noticed it in the winter when there was a constant call for heat, but when summer came and he hit the vent button, the result was more heat. When he hit the air conditioning button there was still more heat. To keep from roasting he opened the driver's side window and the sunroof.

Beads of sweat were forming on Fr. Ross' forehead as he turned the corner in front of the rectory and headed up Oak Street. His first stop was at a yellow duplex on the north end of the street. Hazel Green lived there with her daughter, Katherine. As Fr. Ross knocked and tried the door, he could hear an interview taking place on the EWTN network.

Hazel was sitting in a recliner. Although it was 9:30 a.m. she was still wearing her housecoat. Fr. Ross had a feeling she wore it all day long. He had never seen her in anything different.

"Good morning," he said as he took his accustomed place on the sofa, holding the pyx filled with hosts before him.

"Good morning, Father."

"It's a beautiful day outside. You're going to have to try to sit outside and enjoy it." Fr. Ross knew she wouldn't think of it, but he wanted to offer a positive suggestion.

"I had a bad night, Father. I didn't sleep well. Early this morning my first husband, Harlan, who has been dead 15 years, was standing at the end of the bed. It was a dream but he seemed so real!"

"Yes." Fr. Ross left Hazel free to finish the story without comment.

"He was a mean man who beat me, Father. Life with him was terrible. He drowned."

"I am sorry to hear he wasn't a loving husband."

"He just stood there. He was wearing his old over-coat and the collar was pulled up around his face. He looked as mean as ever, but I wasn't afraid. Somehow I knew he couldn't harm me. His hair was wet and one side of his face was wet and wrinkled. He looked as if he wanted something...perhaps help?

"After he had gone, my second husband appeared, dressed in white. He stood at the foot of the bed, just looking around. He disappeared when I woke up."

Hazel offered no explanation. She just sat there, thinking of the dreams and the memories they evoked.

Fr. Ross was silent also. He thought of another woman who had approached him after Mass to tell him of her dream.

"My sister's husband died at the age of 52," the stranger had told him. It was obvious from the excitement in her voice she had waited the whole Mass to share the story with him.

"He died six months ago. Last week he appeared to her in a dream. He was shining and wearing a new suit. The dream was so real my sister thought he had come back to life. She said, 'Paul, I gave all your clothes away.' Then he answered, 'Don't worry. I am happy. I don't need those clothes.'

"To me," the lady concluded, "it was a sign that he is in heaven." She said it with such conviction that Fr. Ross stopped and re-examined his thoughts about life in the hereafter. By the time he came back to a sense of his present surroundings the lady had disappeared in the crowd. He didn't know her.

Now Hazel Green was telling him about her husbands appearing in a dream. He knew he would spend the rest of the morning wondering about the significance of it all. Were dreams just dreams, or did they contain some message from a world beyond?

Many of his nineteen stops during the day were routine. Some, he felt, weren't even necessary. Lucille Werner, who was ninety-two, couldn't come to church but attended bingo every Tuesday night. "The doctor tells me I have to keep moving," she would say.

"My knee hurts so much," Lucille said as she used a cane to get from the kitchen to the living room. "I don't know what I am going to do."

Invariably, Fr. Ross would meet her in the grocery store later in the day pushing a cart and doing her own shopping.

"This is Mrs. Werner, one of my shut-ins," Fr. Ross would announce to anyone who was near enough to hear. The statement was lost on Mrs. Werner, who smiled and continued on her way. Fr. Ross concluded she just liked the attention.

Such was not the case with the last two visits of the day. Fr. Ross saved them until last so he could spend some time with each of the people.

Lydia Hart had been fighting cancer for two years and Fr. Ross considered her one of his heroes. For the first year she had continued her job as a waitress. Then the time consumed in treatments and pain had forced her to quit her job. She lived with her husband and tried to maintain a normal routine, but it took so much effort. Peeling potatoes for dinner could take the whole morning. She would peel half a potato and then go back to bed to gather the strength to finish the other half. By the time the pan was filled, the morning was gone.

This morning she lay in bed waiting for the doctor to come.

"You can't believe how much pain I am in," she said as Fr. Ross sat by her bed, not knowing what to say.

"It started about 2 o'clock." Lydia winced and rolled the edge of the sheet between her fingers.

"I don't understand why God can't take this pain and divide it among a number of people. No one could believe how it hurts."

It was the first time in two years Fr. Ross had ever heard her complain. He sat there, listening and praying silently, for ten minutes and then reached in his pockets for the oils that he carried on such visits.

"I am going to anoint you," he said as he rose. "Let's

pray that through this anointing Christ may ease some of that pain."

Fr. Ross turned the top off the small brass container of consecrated oil, dipped his thumb in it, and made the sign of the cross on her forehead. "Through this holy anointing may the Lord in His love and mercy help you with the grace of the Holy Spirit. May the Lord, who frees us from sin, save you and raise you up."

He stood there, feeling helpless. Finally he walked back out to the kitchen and spoke to Lydia's husband, who had been waiting in the kitchen. "Keep me informed," Fr. Ross said as he left for his last visit of the day.

Beads of sweat formed on Fr. Ross' forehead again as he drove into the country. He remembered the first time he visited John and Roberta Summers. A parishioner had informed Fr. Ross about the couple. They were Catholic but never went to church. Now they were growing old and perhaps would accept his visit.

When Fr. Ross arrived, they were behind the house in their garden. They couldn't hear unless one shouted directly in their ears. They wore tattered clothes and looked upon his visit as an intrusion. "We will send someone when we want you to visit again. We are not interested in your visits or in receiving communion. At least not weekly," John had said.

Fr. Ross never went back to the farm until after John's death. Now it was one of his weekly stops. He always found Roberta sitting in a wheelchair in the kitchen. An old wood range was standing near a wall but Roberta no longer used it. Instead, she warmed her food on a hot plate that sat on a wooden box in front of her. Whoever took care of her arranged the food she was to prepare on the benches and boxes that surrounded her. Roberta's clothes were virtually rags. The kitchen was filthy. It seemed little more than a prison to which she was confined. Fr. Ross often wondered how she went to the bathroom or got into bed.

"Hello." Fr. Ross cupped his hand and yelled right in

her ear.

She looked at him with washed out blue eyes.

"I will give you communion!" Fr. Ross shouted again. She didn't respond and Fr. Ross didn't know what else to say. He held out the host and placed it on her tongue. Then he turned and left. He had discussed the case with the county nurse but got nowhere. What was happening seemed so cruel, but he didn't know Roberta's thoughts. He thought of a similar situation in which a lady had been moved from such conditions to a community-based living center with good food and immaculate living quarters. Every time he had visited her she had complained that it just wasn't like home. Thank God, Fr. Ross thought to himself. So often he felt like a bystander when a miracle worker was needed.

"As soon as I eat lunch I'm going to get this heat switch fixed," Fr. Ross vowed as he pulled into the garage, his shirt damp with sweat.

As he entered the church to return the hosts that he hadn't used, Fr. Ross noticed the solitary figure sitting in the front pew on the left side of the church. He remembered him from the brief conversation they had had on the last day of school. After placing the pyx in the tabernacle, Fr. Ross genuflected and walked down into the center aisle beside the young man.

"It isn't often I find a person your age praying in our church at this time of day," he said as a way of opening the conversation.

Jim Elliot remained silent, his eyes fixed on the image of the prophet Elijah.

"Isn't your name Jim? Duke, my janitor, says that he has seen you here in the past. It is not as if he was spying on you. He just happened to notice you."

Fr. Ross took a handkerchief from his pocket to wipe his forehead. The sweat had almost dried. The church felt cool compared to riding in his Fiero.

Jim slowly turned toward Fr. Ross. He seemed to be in a trance. As he began to speak, Fr. Ross noticed a gap where an upper front tooth was missing.

"Yes. My name is Jim. I live with my parents on a farm toward Portage."

"I have often seen your mother come to Mass on Sunday. She seldom speaks to me, but I have noticed her. She seems like a very sincere person." Fr. Ross took the opportunity to sit in the pew in front of Jim. He twisted his body and rested his elbow on the back of the bench so he could look directly at Jim.

"My mother is responsible for my religious training," Jim said. "She always made sure that I got to church and to religion classes. We always had to rely on the neighbors bringing us until I got old enough to drive. Then I brought her. We never missed a Sunday.

"My father hates religion. He says it is all a fairy tale. Not my mom. She really believes. She would never think about becoming involved in church activities other than Mass, but I don't know of anyone who has a deeper belief in God. When she goes home from Mass she is a renewed person. She can take anything Dad hands out. It is where she gets her strength."

"She sounds like a fine person," Fr. Ross stated. "I hope I have the opportunity to get to know her better."

Fr. Ross looked at the young man in front of him. He was wearing a dark red T-shirt and jeans. He seemed too young to be without a front tooth. Strange that he didn't have a bridge or plate. His eyes were blue, but very pale.

"What about yourself?" Fr. Ross asked. "What brings you to church in the middle of the day? Is there something I can help you with?"

Jim looked from Fr. Ross to the stained glass window of Elijah, then he looked directly at Fr. Ross. He held his closed Bible in his left hand. The fingers of his right hand rested on the cover while he ran a nervous thumb over the edge of the pages. Fr. Ross could hear the pages snap against each other like cards being shuffled in a deck.

"God has called me back from Shoel, the land of the dead." Jim spoke softly and hesitantly as if searching for the right words. "In calling me back He has changed my name from Jim to Elijah, just like He changed Simon's to Peter. He has given me a mission.

"Elijah challenged the 450 false prophets of Baal. He told them that if they were real prophets they could light the wood around the altar on fire. They couldn't do it! But Elijah could. Elijah did!" Jim thumbed the pages of the Bible for emphasis. "He had the power of God!

"Now the Voice speaks to me," Jim said glancing up at the stained glass window. "This is the mountain where the Lord has invited me and Moses and Elijah. God has made me the new Elijah. The ancient Elijah reaches down and touches me. 'Arise,' he says, 'and do not be afraid.'"

Jim opened his Bible to the passage he wished to read. "Elijah indeed is to come and will restore all things. But I say to you that Elijah has already come, and they did not know him, but did to him what they wished. So also shall the Son of Man suffer at their hands."

The Bible snapped closed and Jim spoke with passion. "My father, Ed, does to me as he wishes. He does not recognize my coming again. Others will follow him. But Jesus has taken me to the mountain and transformed me into the new Elijah. I must purify the land of false prophets and restore all things. I am to light the cleansing fire!

"Others have failed to recognize me as the new Elijah. When I have cried out, they have beaten me. This tooth that is gone is a sign of the mistreatment I have suffered for being the new Elijah. But I am the new Elijah.

"Jesus died at age 33. I was born on July third. July is the seventh month. Three is a holy number. Seven is a holy number. I have been chosen by God."

Fr. Ross listened quietly. He was sure it was the same voice he had heard in the confessional. Yet he knew that he could not make any reference to those conversations without breaking the seal of confession. Besides, what good would it do to interrupt? Jim was lost in his own world. To interrupt would only risk a confrontation.

The rising fire in Jim's eyes and voice made Fr. Ross uneasy. Anger boiled within him, surfacing in his proclamation to be the new Elijah. Not knowing how to handle the situation, Fr. Ross thought it best to walk away from it, for now.

"I don't know what to think of it all," Fr. Ross said. "Perhaps it would be better if I left you to pray." With that he walked down the aisle and out the front door of the church. He was on the sidewalk between the church and rectory when he heard the church door push open. Turning, he saw Jim standing at the top of the steps.

"Are you a man of God?" Jim cried out, his arm and the finger of one hand raised as a craggy old prophet might have done. "Are you a man of God?" he demanded.

"I hope I am," Fr. Ross said.

"Prove yourself."

"All I can say is that I was ordained years ago by Bishop O'Connor and have been assigned to serve at St. Bridget's. I have always wanted to be a priest. It was something I began thinking about when I was in grade school. I have always felt it was God's call."

"I have been called," Jim shouted from the top of the steps. "Elijah has just appeared to me in church. He has told me that you must die on Friday, July third, and rise from behind the altar in the nude on Sunday." With that he turned and disappeared down the steps on the other side.

Fr. Ross stood in silence, thinking of the two confessions he had heard from a person proclaiming himself to be called by God. Of a knife being plunged and fires burning an altar. Now the image of Jim standing at the top of the steps was frozen in his mind, as was his question, "Are you called by God?" How did anyone know for sure? One prayed that he was and tried to act accordingly, but there had never been a voice from heaven that said, "This is my beloved Son, upon whom my favor rests."

The thought of dying on July third haunted him. What had Jim meant? Was it merely the words of a disturbed person or was there something real in the threat? Had the date of Jim's birth and a Friday, symbolic of Good Friday, become something significant in Jim's mind? Was it a veiled threat?

There was a humorous aspect to Jim's pronouncement. If he did rise from behind the altar in the nude on a Sunday, it would certainly get people's attention! Fr. Ross shook his head and laughed as he walked toward the rectory.

12

It was a good season for gardens Fr. Ross thought as he prepared a salad for lunch. Parishioners had given him most of the ingredients. During the winter months his salads were bland, lettuce salads. But now, parishioners were more than happy to bring him their garden excess. If he couldn't eat it all, he discreetly discarded it. It was better to have an abundance than nothing at all.

He sat eating that salad containing a variety only summer brought, topped with a vinegar and oil dressing. It was early summer and gardens were just beginning to mature. It would only get better! For the simple lettuce salads bought in the winter at Zinke's Market, there was nothing like the original Western dressing. But now, a vinegar and oil or Italian dressing was all he needed to accent the taste of the fresh vegetables in the bowl before him.

He had already glanced through the Life section of USA Today and was reading the Sports section when the phone rang. Fr. Ross held on to the newspaper in case the call was one that required that he listen and not reply.

"F..a..thur." It was Rose Wells.

Fr. Ross scanned the headlines of the articles. *"F..a..thur,* this is Rose."

"Hi, Rose. What can I do for you?"

"F..a..thur, do you know what I heard at work yesterday?"

"No. I have no idea what you heard at work."

"Shirley Simons says that two of the ladies who work with me are lesbians, and that everybody in town knows it. One of them goes to our church."

"I would be very careful about making an accusation like that."

"But *F..a..thur,* it's true. How could I be so dumb? Don't you want to know who it is?"

"No, Rose, I honestly don't. If I were you, I would just forget it."

"You know, I think my third husband was homosexual. I never would have guessed it when I was going with him, but once we got married, he never wanted to have sex."

"Maybe he just got old," Fr. Ross suggested. "If I remember correctly, he was seventy when you married him."

Not only was he seventy. He was dying. Fr. Ross remembered when they had come to see him a month before his death. The man had sat in one of the chairs in the office, unable to speak, while Rose dominated the conversation. Finally, Fr. Ross had asked Rose to direct her attention to her husband, who was terminally ill.

"Why am I so dumb?" asked Rose. "I should have guessed those ladies were lesbians."

"Rose, if I were you, I wouldn't be spreading any rumors about people you work with. You could end up in a lot of trouble."

"But *F..a..thur.*"

"Goodbye, Rose."

Fr. Ross went back to reading the sports page. Within minutes the phone rang again.

"St. Bridget's, Fr. Ross speaking."

"Fr. Ross?"

"Yes." Fr. Ross always wondered why people asked when he had already identified himself.

"This is Jim Elliot."

"Yes, Jim." Fr. Ross lifted his eyes from the sports page. "Did you know that I am a veteran?"

"No, I didn't, Jim."

"The Army wanted to fry my brain. They wanted to put me to sleep and send enough electricity through my brain to light a 50-watt light bulb."

"When was this, Jim?"

"It doesn't matter when it was. They were not going to fry my brain. The doctors said it wouldn't hurt, that I would never remember a thing. That was it. They wanted to rob me of the memory of who I am, that I am the new Elijah."

"What hospital did you go to, Jim?"

"That is not important. I wouldn't sign. No one was going to fry my brain!"

"Jim, would you ever think of seeing a doctor? I really think you should."

"I have a doctor and he says there is nothing wrong with me. I talked to him on the phone this afternoon and he says I am in very good health."

"Jim, what is his name? What hospital is he with?"

"I'm not telling you. You'll call him and fill him with lies."

There was a pause. Then Jim began to speak again. "When I was in church, I saw the devil rise from beneath the foot of the angel in the window. He rose and hid in the vigil light stand. Then, as I watched, the whole stand burst into flames like the bush before Moses in the desert. The devil and his friends danced among the flames that belched from the smoky darkness. Everything stopped, and the devil spoke to me with a voice that thundered from a mouth that looked like a black cave. He said that you are one of them. That you are a priest of Baal, an enemy of the truth! The devil said that you had been sent to earth from hell to destroy the kingdom of God.

"Elijah came out of the opposite window and drove Satan away. In the calm that followed, Elijah said that you must die on July third. There are three persons in the Trinity. Jesus was thirty-three years old. I must be the messenger because my mother was thirty-three years old when I was born.

"Elijah, who came down from the window, then led me to the baptismal font beneath his window and poured water on me and anointed me with the power to fulfill this mission. You must die and rise!"

He heard the click as Jim suddenly hung up. He shouldn't let the past confessions influence him, but they did. Now Fr. Ross was frightened; he had lost all interest in eating.

He moved to his front office and sat motionless behind the desk trying to decide on a course of action. Somehow he had to find out if Jim had ever been hospitalized and, if so, which hospital and what was the name of his doctor. The only possible way of doing that was by talking to his mother. Pulling the phone book from a desk drawer, he paged through it until he found the Elliot's number, then reached for the phone and dialed.

A woman's voice answered on the second ring.

"Is this the Elliot's?"

"Yes." The voice seemed hesitant.

"Krista?"

"Yes."

"This is Fr. Michael Ross at St. Bridget's. I often see you in church, although I don't know if we have ever had the opportunity to sit and talk."

"Bernice and Elmer Evans bring me to church when I can get there. I can't always make it. There was a time when I came every week. That was when my son, Jim, was at home."

"Your son is the reason I'm calling. I understand he has returned after being gone for a number of years." Fr. Ross paused. There was silence. It was as if Krista sensed the direction the conversation was going to take and was reluctant to talk.

"It seemed so long," Krista spoke softly.

"I don't know how long he has been home, but in the last few days he has been here at St. Bridget's. I am very worried about him. I think he needs help."

"He was such a good boy, Father. When he went to school he studied hard. He enjoyed reading. He was very religious. He took me to church every Sunday. One year he wanted a Bible for Christmas. That Bible became his most important possession. He was always reading it and quoting it. Sometimes people would make fun of him for doing it, but he didn't care."

"Krista, I know he was a good boy and that he took care of you. Duke, my janitor, has told me all about how good Jim was to you. Duke told me that he brought you to church and that he hunted for food and got a job so he could give you money. He did everything that a loving son could, but something has gone wrong. I am sure you still love him and would like to help him be that loving son again."

Fr. Ross paused, waiting for Krista to respond. He could hear her sobbing. "I would do anything," Krista said softly. "I pray every night that this will go away and he can be my son again. I just don't know where to turn. He changed so much while he was gone. I don't know what happened. Now all he does is fight with my husband. He claims he sees people in the wallpaper. He becomes so angry."

"He told me that he has been seeing a doctor. Do you know if he has? It is important that I talk to his doctor."

"I don't know if he has a doctor. He never tells me where he goes when he leaves. I don't know who it would be."

"He talks about the Army trying to fry his brain. Would he ever have seen a psychiatrist? Maybe even before he disappeared from home?"

"When he first came home from the Army, he took some sort of medicine, but then he stopped taking it.

He said it was a dangerous drug and that the doctors were trying to ruin his mind."

"Do you think it was something a psychiatrist might have recommended?"

"Jim never said."

"Would he have told your husband?"

"No. Never. If my husband knew he was going to a psychiatrist, he would have thrown him out of the house. Real men, he would have said, don't go to shrinks. He would never let Jim have any peace if he knew something like that. Real men fight in the Army; cowards go to psychiatrists."

"Krista, I appreciate your talking to me. I want you to know that I want to help Jim. I think he desperately needs help. May I call you again?"

"Yes, but if my husband answers, please don't say anything about Jim. It will only make things worse."

"I promise I won't."

"Father?"

"Yes."

"Please help Jim. I don't know where to turn. I talked to Dan Iverson at the police station, but I haven't heard from him since. Father, I love Jim. I don't want anything to happen to him. He's all I've got."

Fr. Ross hung up the phone and looked out the window at the Shrine to the Blessed Mother. The candles before the statue burned softly in the mid-afternoon heat. He studied their glow in the red glass for a long time and then rose, walked through the house, and out the side door toward the garage. He sat in the quiet of the Fiero for a few more moments before starting it. Maybe it was time to talk to Dan Iverson.

The police station was one block away. Fr. Ross stopped in front of it. The door of the Fiero squeaked as he got out. Have to oil that hinge, he thought to himself. He noticed that Dan's squad car was in its reserved parking spot. Hopefully, he wouldn't have to wait or go looking for him. Finding Iverson at this time of the year could be an impossible task.

"Is Dan in?" Fr. Ross asked Wanda as he walked in. Wanda Harvey was a parishioner who was quite active in the church.

"Yes, I think he is in his office. Go on back. He won't mind."

Fr. Ross walked down the corridor between the conference rooms. The deputy's office was empty. He glanced at the barred door at the end of the corridor and thought of the only time he had been beyond. He had been called in the middle of the night to come and talk to a priest who had been driving while under the influence of alcohol or drugs. It was one of those touchy situations where it was important for the pastor to help without word getting all over town.

"Dan?" Fr. Ross stood outside Iverson's door and looked in at the tall, lean figure seated behind the desk. Papers stacked everywhere on the desk bore witness to the time of year. It would take winter to bring some semblance of order to the top of that oak desk.

"Fr. Ross, what brings you here? We're so busy this time of year that our paths rarely cross." Iverson took some papers off a nearby chair and pulled it over to Fr. Ross.

"Something is happening and I don't know if it is a problem or not, but I have to talk to somebody. At least share it. Maybe it is nothing and then again...." Fr. Ross took his comb from his pocket and ran it through his hair as he sat down.

Fr. Ross studied Dan's deeply furrowed face. Iverson may have grown old, but he was no one to fool with, he still had the instincts of a fox. "Do you know a young man named Jim Elliot?"

"Yes, in fact, his mother was in here not long ago." Iverson stopped. It was obvious that he wasn't going to divulge any of the conversation unless he thought it was necessary.

"He has been coming to church, and his behavior, to say the least, has been bizarre. I am sure he has a severe mental disorder. The figures in the stained glass windows come alive in his mind. He calls himself the new Elijah and spends a lot of time in front of the window that contains the prophet's picture. On the opposite side of the church is a window depicting the angel casting Satan into hell. Jim sees Elijah moving and talking to him. Satan comes down from the window and dances in the flames of the vigil lights."

"Which matches many of the things his mother says," Iverson said softly, putting his elbows on his desk and his long intertwined fingers beneath his chin. He remembered his encounter with Jim in the restaurant and knew he should be doing something about his strange behavior, but it was summer and he was extremely busy. It was all he and his two deputies could do to keep up with the most flagrant violations. Winter was the time for checking into the problems of the local citizens and running background checks on someone like Jim Elliot. After Labor Day the city emptied, and things became so quiet there was even time to look for lost dogs and cats.

"His mother said he had been gone for a period of time and just isn't the same. I remember Jim from the days when I helped with the Portage boxing program. His dad considered himself a great boxer and wanted his son to follow in his footsteps. Jim wasn't too bad. I felt sorry for him and his mother though. The dad was one step above being a bum. Had him as an overnight guest out back once in a while. Haven't seen him now that he has gotten older and slowed down.

"At any rate Bernice Evans brought Krista here. Krista says it's a real shouting match at home. Jim is constantly quoting the Bible and seeing the devil in the wallpaper in his bedroom.

"The day she was here, she and Bernice had followed him into town. They found him in church that day and had talked him into getting in the car to go home, but he jumped out and disappeared.

"I tracked him down. Didn't get very far with him. He got loud and talked about doctors trying to fry his brain.

Then he started yelling about not being able to get a job."

"I know," Fr. Ross stated. "I've heard it all. I worry about that, but what has frightened me is a threat that he made. He gets going on all these numbers and says he has been baptized for a mission. The mission is to put me to death as a false priest. I don't want you to laugh, but he says I am going to die and rise from the dead from behind the altar in the nude." Fr. Ross almost laughed himself. What was he doing here? But somehow the mixture of those secret confessed murders and the confrontation over the telephone frightened him.

"Father, I agree that Jim has definite mental problems, but I have problems too. This is the busiest time of the year. We've got the Fourth of July coming up, and that is the busiest weekend of all. My hands are tied. State law says that unless he does something violent to himself or someone else, I can't touch him. He could commit himself for observation, but even then he can sign himself out and walk free. I'm sorry, but that's where it stands."

"In other words we have to wait until he kills someone before we can do anything?"

"I don't know if it goes that far. If he started standing in the middle of the street saying he is a spirit that cars can drive right through without harming, we may have something."

Iverson shifted in his oak swivel chair. He knew the law and how, in this case, the individual was protected.

"I know I shouldn't be scared, but something deep within has me on edge. I don't like being threatened, especially by someone like Jim Elliot. You can't reason with him. I've never been in this position before."

Iverson wasn't going to add to his fears by telling Fr. Ross that Jim had been an excellent marksman in the Army. It probably wasn't significant anyway. "Tell you what, Father, when we get through the Fourth of July, I'll look into it."

"You know the third of July is the day I'm supposed to die. That's the mission he says he has been baptized for."

"Like I said, we can't do anything because of what he says. I am sure he is either manic-depressive or schizophrenic, but he has to do something violent to himself or another person. The law protects such people from just being rounded up and institutionalized."

"As I am learning, but it is me he is after."

"If it is any comfort, such people seldom turn thought into action."

"I hope you are right, but this might be the exception." Fr. Ross rose from his chair and thanked Dan for taking the time to talk with him. It was those confessions that worried him. Were they also the outbursts of mental illness, figments of the imagination? He didn't know, but he did not want to be the subject of Jim's next confession.

13

The red sun was setting over the woods behind the Elliot farm. The days of the summer were long, and Krista enjoyed going out after supper and spending the remaining hours of the day in her garden. There were those early mosquitoes, but the heat of the day had passed. Besides, there was the beauty of a sun that could turn the trees on the horizon black and then, within a few moments, be gone. The reds and yellows lingered but soon it would be dark.

Krista stayed until the last traces of red were gone. The garden had become her refuge from the insanity that filled her house. What could she do? The only two people who could do something, Dan Iverson and Fr. Ross, knew what was happening. There was no one else to tell, no one else to go to. She had to be patient.

All traces of light vanished and it was time to face the wars that were being waged within her house and her son's mind. Using her hoe as a cane, Krista forced her short, bowed legs into motion. If only God would give her strength.

She stepped on the porch and leaned the hoe against the wall. Jim and Ed were in a heated conversation. The door squeaked as she entered but neither man noticed her.

"If I were younger, I'd whip you!" Ed shouted. "I'd thrash you to within an inch of your life." Ed rocked back and forth and spat at the coffee can on the floor. The brown juice missed, but Ed couldn't have cared less. He was turned sideways in the rocker, waving a deformed hand at Jim. "I'd kick your ass."

"You couldn't do anything," taunted Jim, who was seated at the table. "I have the power now. I have the power to destroy or let live. I have the power of Elijah! You are nothing but an old man trapped in a rocking chair. Now I have the power!"

Krista shuffled across the room and put her arm on Jim's shoulder, trying to rub the rage from his body.

"Leave him alone, Jim," she said. "What he did is in the past. He can't hurt you now. He's just an old man waiting in his chair to die."

"But he still remembers," said Jim. "He remembers, and he enjoys those memories."

Krista continued to rub her son's shoulder. A tear rolled down her cheek and dropped onto Jim's T-shirt.

"It isn't worth it," Krista whispered. "You're letting him destroy you." Her tears flowed freely now. Jim's shoulder quivered beneath her hand. She placed her other hand on the opposite shoulder. If only she could blot out the anger. "Jim. I love you. Can't you let it be? What would it take to turn you back into the person I once knew? I pray and I pray and I pray.... You are my only son, my only hope, my only joy. I love you, Jim. Please...."

Jim said nothing, giving his attention to the open Bible on the table before him. He turned a page, glanced at it, and then turned another.

Krista looked over Jim's shoulder at the Bible. What had happened to the boy who had loved God's message so much? Where was she ever going to find help for him? She looked across the room at the picture of Christ hanging on the wall, her lips moving silently as she said another prayer for her son.

Jim put his hand on the table and slid sideways out of the chair. Without speaking he left the kitchen and began walking up the stairs to his bedroom. Suddenly he felt very cold. How could that be? His argument with his father had left him sweating just minutes before. It was the end of June and it had been a hot, muggy day. The house wasn't air-conditioned. It couldn't cool down that fast. Yet, as he walked down the hall toward his bedroom he found himself rubbing his hands together to warm them. The closer he came to his room, the colder it got. He opened the door and stepped inside. He shivered. The skin on his shoulders and biceps rose in needle points. His teeth chattered.

What was it? Jim expected to hear the Voice but there was only the silence of a mid-winter's moonlit eve. He expected to see figures dancing in the wallpaper but the walls were covered with frost. The icy crystals shimmered in the glow of the bare bulb overhead.

Backing slowly from the room, Jim turned and ran down the hall and stairs toward the kitchen. His father rocked in angry silence while his mother sat crying at the table. Jim stood motionless, staring at his father. He could hear the ticking of the antique wall clock. Each movement of the pendulum and every sound that accompanied it took an eternity. Then it seemed as if a great thawing took place. His body warmed, and sounds returned to normal.

Suddenly Jim realized the source of the cold. It wasn't his bedroom. It was his father.

"What is it?" Krista asked Jim. "What is happening?"

Jim turned and looked at Krista. The fiery, wild-eyed

look was one she would never forget. Whatever it was, he would never share the experience with her. The devil that had captured her son shared no secrets.

14

Rocky's Auto Salvage was four miles south of Portage on Highway 51. It was an old-fashioned junkyard. Behind the chain link fence was a storefront surrounded by metal buildings and lean-tos. An old wrecker, rusted yard trucks, and customers' cars were crowded into the space between the office and front fence.

On a busy day, driving in one gate and out the other was almost impossible. Cars stacked three high filled the slopes behind the buildings. A marsh served as the back boundary.

Fr. Ross was a frequent customer, looking for replacement parts for his vehicles. While he hated shopping, he had always enjoyed browsing through a good junkyard. It dated back to when his grandfather, a blacksmith by trade, took him along to the local yard looking for parts to use in his shop. There was a special building in which, from time to time, they found metal toys. It was always the last shed they visited, and if they found a toy, Fr. Ross' grandfather bought it for him. He still had that special John Deere toy tractor his grandfather had bought and then made equipment for in his blacksmith shop. His childhood friends envied him for having that tractor and enough machinery to operate a fantasy farm.

Fr. Ross enjoyed the people who worked at Rocky's. None of them went to his church but over the years they had become his friends. They and the yard had inspired many of Fr. Ross' sermons. Rocky, the bearded proprietor, often gave Fr. Ross a discount because he sent so much business his way.

Entering the office was intimidating. The employees

said nothing. They stared stone-faced from their positions behind the counter and along the row of battered bar stools that stood in front of the counter. An old chocolate Labrador opened one eye as it rested on a ragged brown sofa, seeming to defy anyone to disturb its rest. A Harley Davidson motorcycle sat in the middle of the room. Stacks of tires and rims stood on the floor. Batteries and assorted auto parts rested against the wall and front counter. A soda machine stood along the back wall. No one ever put a coin directly into the machine. Instead, they put the money in the cash register and opened the front door of the machine by turning the key.

A family of kittens scrambled wildly as Fr. Ross entered the office. He was greeted by Hank Retzloff, "You mean we can't say 'God damn ass hole?'" It was obvious they had seen Fr. Ross approaching. Hank, nicknamed "The Pervert", had become a special friend of Fr. Ross'. Their friendship dated back to a day when Hank was out in the yard helping Fr. Ross get a part for his car. Rocky had sent another worker out to get something from a nearby car. "Rocky wants to know how the priest and the pervert are doing," the worker had said on his way to his destination.

The Pervert lived in a small trailer on the property. Fr. Ross had never seen it, but if Hank's appearance matched the trailer, it was a disaster. His sunken cheeks were covered by a beard that got shaved every other week at the most. His black hair was pushed up under his hat. "I wear the hat so I don't have to wash my hair," Hank had confided to Fr. Ross on one visit. His eyes were a washed-out blue. He wore a western-style shirt and Levis with boots.

"I'm a heathen," Hank announced one day. Still, Fr. Ross considered him one of those special people who existed in his life. If Hank did any work for him, he always got a tip. At Christmas Fr. Ross always slipped an envelope into his shirt pocket, even though Hank told him it was a day just like any other day. Somehow Fr.

Ross knew that wasn't a true statement. People like Hank just drifted away from their churches and didn't know how to return. Deep inside there was a faith waiting to surface. The official church was missing one of its callings, Fr. Ross felt. It was too busy taking care of itself and those already comfortably within it to reach out for people like Hank.

"Hank," Fr. Ross said in feigned surprise and disgust as he entered the office. He was aware that all the silent stares were aimed in his direction.

Fr. Ross saw Rocky sitting on his favorite stool behind the counter. His bearded face was framed by the cash register on one side and stacks of parts on the other. A dirty black phone receiver rested on his shoulder. At times it seemed to disappear in Rocky's shaggy beard. One word, "Rocky's," was grunted into the phone intermittently. Then one of the workers got off a stool to retrieve a part for a customer who promised to stop by later. Often it was easier and quicker to bring your own tools and remove the part yourself.

Rocky's blue-green eyes focused on Fr. Ross. Without interrupting the phone conversation he acknowledged the priest's presence with a nod.

"Need a pair of tires," Fr. Ross said, not expecting an answer. He turned to Hank. "I need a pair of tires for the Fiero."

Hank got off his stool and led Fr. Ross out the front door and around the corner of the building, stopping at the rear of the office building to point out a new lean-to he had built for transmissions. "Said some awful words when I smashed a finger with a hammer," Hank confessed as he held his bandaged finger out for inspection. "You can still see the trail of blood up on the roof." Then, as they continued on their way, Hank said, "I thought about being a carpenter, but then I thought of what they did to Jesus and decided to be a welder."

Fr. Ross smiled.

Inside the metal shed where the tires were stored the two searched the racks until they found a pair that would fit the Fiero. While Hank got them down, Fr. Ross went to get his car. After Hank changed the tires, they returned to the office and Fr. Ross paid Rocky.

"Just remember," Fr. Ross said. "If Hank goes to jail this winter, I'm going to go and ask that he be put in my custody. I've got a room in the church basement we can turn into an apartment."

It was an ongoing joke. Hank had spent the past two winters in jail for getting behind in paying child support. "I knew her long enough to get her pregnant," Hank had once told Fr. Ross about his short time as a married man. After his last stay in jail he had managed to get the payments reduced to seventeen dollars a month. "I'll be ninety-three when I get done paying.

They will have to come to my grave to get those last payments!" Hank had it all calculated. He knew how to beat the system.

"Someday I'm going to surprise you and come and sit in the front row during one of your services," the Pervert said as Fr. Ross turned to leave.

"I'd love it," Fr. Ross spoke the truth. It would be a great day in his life if that ever happened.

Duke Lonergan brought the riding lawn mower to a halt and shut it off as Fr. Ross pulled into the garage behind the rectory. He lifted his Foxy's Sportsman's Bar hat and adjusted the strands of gray hair beneath. It was his day to do the yard work around the buildings. There wasn't much lawn. The lot behind the school and the one on the north side of the church were paved. It was just a matter of mowing the narrow strips between the buildings, sidewalks, and parking lots, and keeping the hedges trimmed.

Duke had already trimmed the hedges and was doing the last of the lawn when Fr. Ross arrived. A chat with Fr. Ross meant he could put off vacuuming, dusting, and cleaning the bathrooms until after lunch. Duke turned sideways on the mower as Fr. Ross closed the garage door.

Seven steps brought Fr. Ross to the side of the lawn

mower. He took his comb from his pocket and whisked it through his hair before speaking.

"All done?"

"Just this piece to go."

Then there was silence as they both studied the uncut grass that would require, at most, one pass down and back. Fr. Ross noted that grass had stuck to Duke's high-topped work shoes.

"Have you seen Jim Elliot around here?" Fr. Ross asked.

"From time to time," Duke said, resting his hands on the steering wheel.

"What's he been doing?"

Duke sensed the conversation was going to be a long one. "Sometimes he drives through the cemetery. Sometimes he just sits in church. One day I caught him in the basement of church beside the door to the tunnel that goes under the street to the school. I asked him what he was doing and he said he was going to the bathroom, but the bathrooms are at the bottom of the steps."

"Has he been doing anything else strange?"

Duke fished his pack of Salems from his shirt pocket and flipped one loose. He put the cigarette in his mouth and struck a match, cupping the burning flame in his hand. When the end of the cigarette glowed red, Duke continued, "Lot of things." The words and the inhaled smoke came forth in the same breath. "One day I was at the stop sign down here on Oak Street and he was talking to the light. Said something about the devil trying to trick him by switching the light to red just as he was going to cross. He was out of it if you ask me."

"Duke, he has me scared. I've dealt with a lot of unusual people, but there is something different about Elliot."

Duke thought back to that Saturday night at the Cove when he had told Chris Walker that Fr. Ross had seemed preoccupied. So this was it.

"I've even talked to Dan Iverson about it," Fr. Ross

said. "The guy thinks he is Elijah the prophet."

"He spends a lot of time in front of that window," Duke interjected.

"He didn't say he was going to kill me, but he says I'm going to die on July third. Jim says it's his birthday."

Duke studied his cigarette and the yellow stains on his fingers.

"I called his mother and she broke down. He returned from a mysterious trip a totally different person. She doesn't know what to do. Seems Jim and her husband are constantly fighting."

"I heard his mother came to church looking for him one day," Duke said.

"I talked to Iverson. He says he can't do anything until after the Fourth. But I'm telling you, I'm worried. It's gotten to where I lock my bedroom door at night."

"Anything you think I should do?" Duke thought of his dream. He had had it again. Those cassocks with hoods proceeding toward the light. Fr. Ross the only recognizable face. Sensing Fr. Ross wasn't going to return. Should he tell Fr. Ross? No. It would just add to his worries.

"What can you do? Nothing really. Maybe it is just me. You know, St. Bridget, the patron saint of this parish, was forever having visions and warning popes and kings about the lives they were leading. Some of the visions involved the passion of Christ. Of course, the people of the time weren't too happy with her. Some thought she was crazy. Maybe it goes with the territory. Sometimes I think this parish attracts the same sort of people. Visionary nuts!"

The conversation was interrupted by the arrival of Dan Iverson's squad car.

"Been trying to call you," said Iverson as he swung the door open and stepped out. "Tourist from Indiana had a heart attack on the Upper Dells boat trip. They were at Witches Gulch when it happened. He was dead by the time the ambulance got there. The ambulance is down at the Nickolai Funeral Home. The widow wants you to come and anoint him before they do anything."

Fr. Ross turned back toward the garage. He always kept an extra set of oils for anointing the sick in his car. He knew the prayers by heart. The Nickolai Funeral Home was only a half block away and it wouldn't take long for him to get there.

The funeral home was a large, white residential building that had been converted to its present use a generation ago. The owner, Fritz Nickolai, met Fr. Ross on the porch.

"I'm glad Dan could find you," Fritz said as he shook Fr. Ross' hand. "The deceased was from Indiana. He and his wife are retired and on vacation. The boat had just docked at Witches Gulch, and the passengers were being guided through the passageways when it happened. He just dropped over. One of the workers tried to revive him but couldn't. He was dead before the ambulance arrived. His name is Luke Dimaggio, and his wife's name is Kathryn. Why don't you come in the office and I'll introduce you to Kathryn? Some way to end a vacation!"

The office was a small room just inside the entrance. As Fr. Ross looked in he saw Kathryn sitting in a chair beside Fritz's desk. Her gray hair was disheveled from the number of times she had run her fingers through it. Her eyes were red from crying. She held a ragged Upper Dells boat guidebook in her hands.

"Thank you for coming," she whispered.

"I'm just happy that the police found me so quickly," Fr. Ross said.

They both sat still for a moment, and then Fr. Ross broke the silence.

"I'll go and anoint Luke, then I'll come back."

Fr. Ross walked back out into the glaring sun. As he reached the Dells ambulance he noticed that Mike Weber, his orange paramedic jacket thrown on over his blue jeans and plaid shirt, was standing by the rear door waiting for him. Mike worked as an independent carpenter and was free to respond to such calls and stay as long as necessary. Those who had answered the call with him had already returned to work.

Mike silently opened one of the double doors at the back of the van and Fr. Ross stepped up inside. Luke's body was still strapped to the gurney. It was covered with a white sheet. Fr. Ross stood hunched over the body for a moment. He reached into his pocket for the leather pouch that held three brass thimble-sized containers. He opened the one that contained the oil for the infirm. Then he placed the leather pouch and two other containers on a stainless steel ledge on the side of the ambulance.

Fr. Ross turned back toward the gurney and lifted the sheet from Luke's head. Luke's skin had already become waxen and his face had lost most of its color. The white plastic tube placed in his mouth and down his esophagus to ventilate the lungs, remained in place. Luke's tongue protruded between his lips beside the tube. The cord that held the tube in place had pulled his left ear forward and folded it over. Luke's eyes had been closed.

Fr. Ross studied Luke's most distinguishing feature, a hawk-like nose, and tried to envision how he had looked in the fullness of life. He paused for a moment to reflect on his own mortality. Then he dipped his thumb into the container. As he made the sign of the cross on Luke's forehead he prayed, "Through this holy anointing may the Lord in His love and mercy help you with the grace of the Holy Spirit. May the Lord, who frees you from sin, save you and raise you up."

After he placed the oils back into their leather pouch, Fr. Ross turned back toward the body. In the silence of the ambulance he said his own prayer for Luke and his widow. The trip back to Indiana would not be an easy one for Kathryn. The ultimate sadness had disrupted what was to have been a trip filled with the happiness of retired life.

Saying a prayer to the Holy Spirit for the wisdom to speak, Fr. Ross returned to the funeral home to visit with Kathryn and see if he could be of any help. Death scenes and funerals were never pleasant but he found them some of the most rewarding times in his ministry. His reputation for doing well in difficult times meant that Catholics and non-Catholics came to him in the most desperate of situations.

Fr. Ross remembered a time when a protester committed suicide by pouring gasoline on his clothes and igniting it. The person had not belonged to any of the churches in the area. Fr. Ross was asked if he would conduct a funeral service after all the other ministers in town had turned down the request. The body had been burned so badly it was impossible for the funeral director to prepare it properly. As Fr. Ross stood at the lectern conducting the service at the funeral home, he could smell the charred remains through the nearby closed casket.

"You always get the tough ones," Fritz Nickolai had told him when it was over.

"I'm sort of like Dirty Harry," Fr. Ross answered. He was proud of the fact that people would turn to him in moments like that.

After helping Kathryn make arrangements for taking Luke back to Indiana, Fr. Ross headed back to the rectory. As he drove, he thought of their conversation.

"The day we were married was windy, and my aunt said that people who marry on a windy day have a stormy marriage," Kathryn had said. "Ours was a stormy marriage, but he always stuck up for me and I always stuck up for him." Fr. Ross had never heard the statement before.

It was now three o'clock in the afternoon. Since he had missed lunch again, Fr. Ross decided to carry a cup of coffee and an orange and banana to his office. He put them on his desk and ran a comb through his hair. Then he slid forward in his chair and put the comb back in his pocket.

He ate the fruit, took a deep drink of coffee and began to look through the mail. He always took out the first class mail first. Anything with a hand-written address received his immediate attention. He opened bills next, then addressographed advertisements last, if at all.

As he took another drink of coffee he noticed a letter addressed to him in pencil. There was no return address. It was postmarked Wisconsin Dells.

Fr. Ross ran a letter opener along the top of the envelope and removed a letter written on blue-lined notebook paper torn from a spiral binder. It began with a simple, "*Fr. Ross.*" The hand-written message continued:

I have prayed to God, asking if you are a true priest. The reason for concern is to be at the hands of a priest because I need God's strength and the counseling of Our Father's holiest men. I need not make one mistake with Our Father's most precious gift of life.

I believe in the Creator of Heaven and Earth. I believe in Jesus Christ, His only begotten Son of the Most Blessed Virgin Mary. I believe in the sacrament of Holy Communion, the forgiveness of sin, and eternal life. Can you imagine eternity?

There is most assuredly an everlasting hell. Our Father has forgiven my sins and I will dwell in the house of the Lord forever and ever. Amen. I believe in the baptism of forgiveness of sins. Our Father forgave me of my sins on June 9...three, three, three.

I pray the non-believers think I was mad. Had a nervous breakdown. Father, I was saved. I have heard the voice of God. He speaks to me now.

Father, you are lax. You are no shepherd. You best get down on your knees. You make me sick. Yes, the bishop will be talking to you. I have spoken with his secretary and written him a letter.

I am going to tell the newspapers and the television stations about you. Get your act, and I mean act, together. Christ was crucified for the truth, Lincoln, J.F.K., Bobby Kennedy, Martin Luther King.

I made ads for WNNO, the radio station in Wisconsin Dells. Duke Lonergan had them pulled off.

I told him if I ever met him in the streets I will beat the shit out of him. He called me and said he would beat me with a tire iron. Now he calls back all night making unintelligible sounds like beware...beware....

I am a truthful person and I speak for God as one of His prophets. I am the new Elijah!

Steroids cured me at one time. I had an adverse reaction to them. I was strapped down. The doctor forced medication down me. They tried to fry my brain but I escaped. This doctor won't practice again. Thanks and Glory be to Our Lord Jesus Christ.

I must not take medications. I must be pure for the Lord. I am Elijah, a divine messenger.

Duke Lonergan will go straight to hell. There is one. Don't you know?

I went to confession to you, but you do not act in the name of God. Jesus cast out demons in the name of God. You say the words of absolution and make a sign of the cross over me and nothing happens. The demons are still there.

You are a false priest running around in the end time. I have been sent by God to test you. You have been found wanting and must be destroyed in flames of wrath on July 3.

I am the prophet Elijah who must foretell the second coming of Christ. I am among the saints who will be caught up in the rapture of the end time. Devils must be eliminated. Evil destroyed. The Church made pure and worthy of the Lamb.

I have tried to tell the world and they have failed to listen. Now I must act!

> *Elijah*

Fr. Ross held the letter in his right hand as he slowly pushed the uneaten end of a banana from side to side on a paper plate with the index finger of his left hand. He didn't feel like eating. He stared at the Blessed Mother shrine in the yard between the church and the rectory. He prayed for guidance and wondered what he should do.

The phone rang.

Fr. Ross let it ring twice before picking it up. If only it had left him to his thoughts.

"F..a..thur."

"F..a..thur. This is Rose Wells."

"Rose."

"F..a..thur. Would you say some prayers for a man I know? My friend's husband was guarding a prisoner at the Oxford Penitentiary for eight hours. The prisoner was sick and threw up all the time. My friend's husband went home and got the chills. He shouldn't have gone back to work but did and had to guard the same prisoner. Now my friend's husband is at the University Hospital in Madison with a mysterious illness. The doctors don't know what it is. They can't ask the doctors at the prison what the prisoner has, because that would be an invasion of privacy. The University Hospital chaplain visited my friend's husband but he is a cold fish. You are OK. I checked you out and the people say you are OK."

"Thanks, Rose."

"But why won't you let me drink out of the cup as well as receive a host at communion? You told me it is not the custom at St. Bridget's and you are worried about germs. If you are worried about germs, why do you let the communion ministers drink from it? Do you know Tony Fredricks is weird?"

"No."

"You let Tony Fredricks drink out of it because he is a communion minister, and I know he's weird. I may not have known my third husband was weird but I know Tony is weird."

"Rose, I've cautioned you about making accusations."

"You let that female teacher with a beard drink from the cup when school is in session and there is a need for a communion minister. You know which one I mean?"

"No. I am afraid I don't," said Fr. Ross. "Rose, are you sure she is a teacher at our grade school?"

"You know the one."

"No. I don't."

"I had to ask who she was. And remember the person I told you about who wanted a husband who could give her a mink and seven million dollars? She is a lesbian. You know her and talk to her."

"Rose. Why do you keep coming to me for advice when I can't identify a homosexual, a lesbian, or a woman with a beard?"

"Because you are OK. You did tell me not to chase men for a year after my husband died, but that is OK. You don't understand. I'm a woman in heat."

"Homo...lesbian...beard...woman in heat. I must say you've made my day. Who was the person you wanted prayed for?"

"...I don't know. After all this I forgot his name. Let me think..."

"When you think of it, call me back."

"F..a..thur."

As Fr. Ross hung up the phone, he could see Duke hurrying up the sidewalk between the church and the rectory. The doorbell rang.

Duke didn't bother to take his hat off as Fr. Ross let him in.

"You've got to come over to church. Jim Elliot is over there, and he says he is going to beat the shit out of me. Says I got some ads he made pulled off WNNO. I don't know what he is talking about."

Fr. Ross followed Duke out of the rectory. As he looked toward the church he could see Jim standing at the top of the steps outside the front doors.

"Don't come any closer!" Jim yelled at them. "You won't believe what happened in there. I had intercourse with the Blessed Mother. I have become divine and was given a mission of fighting the devil. It is going to be a bloody battle but I will prevail."

Fr. Ross and Duke stood motionless.

Waving his Bible and pointing at Duke, Jim continued. "He had my ads pulled off WNNO. I'm going to talk to the owner and do my own talk show."

"Would you go back to the rectory and call Dan Iverson?" Fr. Ross said quietly.

Duke turned and began walking down the sidewalk.

When Fr. Ross turned back toward Jim, he saw him standing with his Bible open.

"Listen to what it says in Matthew's Gospel." Jim held the Bible open in one hand and had the other raised above his head. "Jesus replied, 'Elijah must come and set everything in order. And, in fact, he has already come and wasn't recognized and was badly mistreated by many.'"

Jim pointed to his missing tooth. "They beat me! They beat me!" he screamed.

"Jim, no one wants to mistreat you. We want to help you. Let's go back inside the church and sit for a while."

Fr. Ross started up the steps. He walked past the young man, who turned and looked at the door held open in invitation. Jim's blue eyes were filled with hate. His body trembled beneath the red T-shirt. He hesitated, then followed Fr. Ross into the cool church. Once inside Jim took the lead down the aisle to the front, where he sat down in the pew nearest the stained glass window of Elijah.

No one spoke. Fr. Ross said a silent prayer. Jim seemed calm and his lips moved in a silent prayer of his own. He was paging through his Bible when Dan Iverson and Duke entered the church and walked down the center aisle.

They were standing at the end of the pew when Jim turned. His eyes locked on Iverson's uniform. He said nothing for a moment. There was only the stillness that a church has. Suddenly, Jim's eyes blazed with rage. Before anyone could react, he got up, ran down the side aisle and escaped out the side door to the handicap ramp.

Dan Iverson led the way out of the main doors of the church. As Iverson, Duke and Fr. Ross looked down Oak Street they could see Jim standing in the middle of the street, his arms stretched toward the sky. When he saw them he waved his Bible.

"I am Elijah! I am protected by God."

A car coming up the street screeched to a halt. The driver lowered a window and shouted at Iverson, "What's going on? I could have killed that guy."

"Stay here," Iverson said to Fr. Ross and Duke.

As the two watched, Iverson guided Jim into the back seat of his squad car, which was parked across from the front entrance of the church. Then Dan walked over to the car that had stopped and spoke to the driver before waving him on.

"The law says we can't commit Jim for treatment unless he is a threat to himself or someone else. Hopefully this will be enough to convince the doctors at St. Bede's Hospital in Oshkosh that something should be done. I'm going to take him up there right now."

As Iverson opened the driver's door of the squad car, Jim shouted through the wire that separated the two seats. "I'm not afraid! Death is the path to God. If you kill me, I will sit at the right hand of the Father as His blessed and chosen one."

Fr. Ross could no longer hear his voice, but he could see Jim's face pressed against the rear window of the car as it pulled away. A twisted face filled with the rages of hell stared out at Duke and Fr. Ross.

"Let's hope that's the end of it," Fr. Ross said to Duke as the two crossed the street and walked back toward the rectory.

For Dan Iverson and Jim Elliot the day ended with a two-hour drive to St. Bede's Hospital. Jim had become passive and walked through the front doors of the hospital with Dan in a fashion that left no hint of what had transpired two hours before.

Dan spoke briefly with the secretary. Then Jim and Dan took the elevator to the fourth floor and turned to the left. Double doors separated this ward from the others. Dan looked through a window in one of the doors and pressed a button. A buzzer sounded. A nurse at the far end of the corridor looked up from her work.

Dan could hear the lock on the door release. He pressed the latch and opened the door.

As they walked toward the nurses station, Jim studied the paintings on the wall. He looked in the rooms to see who might be in them. They were standing at the desk when an elderly lady came over from the nearby lounge. She walked slowly and quietly. Without raising a hand she studied Jim and asked, "Have you come to join us for coffee?"

15

At Jim Elliot's direction Roger Smyth, a volunteer at St. Bede's Hospital, turned into the long dirt driveway leading to the farmhouse where Jim lived.

"It is a beautiful setting," Roger said as he surveyed the farm buildings and the trees behind them.

"This has been home for a long time," Jim said. "My parents retired with very little money and fortunately the owner of the buildings is understanding when it comes to rent. The fee is a small one, and if they don't have it, he never says a word. He uses the buildings and the surrounding farmland and lets them live in the house."

Jim didn't mention that the owner felt sorry for his mother because his father spent every cent he earned at the bars. That was why he let them move in and never asked for any rent. They lived on what Jim caught or shot and what was grown in their garden. The farm owner and his wife always looked for used clothing. Whenever they saw something that would fit Jim or his mother, they bought it. It was their form of charity.

Roger stopped his burgundy Buick between the house and the barn. Dust from the driveway dulled its shine. He would have to run it through the car wash when he got back to Oshkosh.

He and Jim stepped from the air-conditioned car into the mid-day heat of summer. They made their way to the edge of the garden. Krista Elliot had seen the strange car coming up the driveway and was slowly making her way toward them from the far side of the garden.

Roger hesitated at the edge of the garden, not wanting to get his shoes dusty. Jim stood beside him. His only luggage was a bag of prescription medicine. The woman Roger saw making her way through the rows of vegetables could have stepped out of a Currier & Ives painting. Her hair was gray and short, her body stocky. Her faded blue apron and cotton print dress had been washed many times. When she walked, Krista lifted each foot as if it were stuck on flypaper. Each step was an effort.

Krista looked at the two figures from a distance. Jim had been gone for three days, but she was growing accustomed to his prolonged absences. Dan Iverson and a deputy had returned Jim's car to the farm and told her that Jim was in the hospital. They didn't tell her why he was in the hospital, except that it wasn't a physical ailment. They told her he needed a rest and he would be home sometime in the future. When she had pressed for more information, Dan said they were trying to calm Jim down and change his behavior so he would no longer rant and rave. Krista didn't know anything about mental health but she had prayed every night that Jim's personality would change.

She looked at the unfamiliar car parked in the yard. Then she recognized Jim. He seemed different, standing there quietly beside the stranger. It reminded her of his grade school days when a neighbor would give him a ride home from school. Jim would always stand in silence while she and the neighbor visited.

"Good morning," the thin gray-haired man began. "My name is Roger Smyth, and I am a volunteer at St. Bede's Hospital in Oshkosh. The hospital asked me to drive your son home."

"Good morning," Krista answered with some apprehension.

"I don't know if he called, but the Wisconsin Dells chief of police, Dan Iverson, brought your son to the hospital three days ago. The hospital asked that I tell you they would like Jim to stay longer so they can work with him, but he refused. Wisconsin state law requires that he be released after three days if those are his wishes. The state is very strict about referrals to this section of Mercy Medical. Unless the person is a threat to himself or someone else, he must commit himself. He's free to leave if he insists. After listening to Police Chief Iverson, the doctors questioned if this was really life-threatening. Jim probably could have left at any time but the doctors did manage to convince him to stay three days.

"Jim suffers from a mental illness that can be controlled by medicine. The doctors felt that they needed more time to work with him and to make sure he is willing to take the medicine. He has enough for three days, but then he'll have to buy some more. The prescription is on the bottle. There's also a phone number on a slip in the bag. If you or Jim have any questions you can call the hospital."

Krista stood motionless and silent. Roger could hear a deer fly buzzing overhead. The silence made him uncomfortable, and to break the spell he turned to Jim and said goodbye.

"Remember, if you have any questions, call the hospital. Don't forget to get the prescription filled in the next day or two."

Jim thanked him for driving him home. Roger began the walk back to his car. Jim turned back to his mother who still stood in the garden, uncertain about what was happening. Her son was home and while he had yet to speak to her, she could sense a great difference. She studied him as he stood at the edge of the garden. He seemed so peaceful. It was her son of old. The miracle she had prayed for had happened.

Jim dropped the bag he was holding and walked between rows of potatoes to where his mother stood. He embraced her. When she finally pulled her head back, there were tear stains on the front of Jim's dark T-shirt.

"It's all right, Mom. I've been in the hospital, but there's nothing to worry about. The doctors told me they wished everyone was as crazy as I am. They didn't find anything wrong with me. The priest, Fr. Claude, told me there was definitely nothing wrong with me. I even went to Mass, and he told me after it was over that if they had filled out any forms forcing me to be there, they should tear them up. Mom, I'm fine."

Krista was still trying to comprehend the dramatic change in her son's mood. The wild expression on his face had been replaced with one of serenity. The fire in his eyes had been replaced with gentleness. There was no anger or hatred in his voice. He was no longer claiming to be a messenger of God. Instead, he seemed to be the loving son she had once known.

"Mom, why don't you just sit while I hoe some of these potatoes?" he said. He walked over to the edge of the garden and picked up the bottom of a press-back chair. Somewhere in its past, the spindles in the back had been broken and then sawed off to form a stool. Krista had taken it to the garden to rest on and work from. Jim brought the chair back to his mother, gently took her by the arm and helped her sit down.

He walked down the row of potatoes and picked up the hoe. As he worked the sandy loam, scraping sounds could be heard from the hoe cutting through the earth and weeds.

Krista sat in silence, watching her son work. Beads of sweat formed on his forehead and spotted his T-shirt. Every mother, parent, watches the child grow, often rebel, and become independent, adult. Then they wait for their return. What will they be like when they return? Will they have turned out to be what the parents hoped and prayed for?

Finally, she got the courage to break the silence. "I have prayed so long for this day, Jim. I don't know what happened, but I hope it's over."

"It doesn't matter now. I'm home."

"I know. I just can't help thinking of how you disappeared... just were gone. Where did you go? What did you do during those years? You will never know how much I prayed for your safety."

"It's not important where I went or what I did, Mom. I'm back. I want to take care of you just like I used to. I love you. We can overcome anything. Remember how you used to tell me that?"

"I remember." Krista's mind swept back over the years. This son standing before her in a field of potatoes had been her only hope on those dark days when she had sworn she was going to leave Ed, even though he said the only way she would leave was in a body bag. This son was the only ray of love in a home that knew no love. He was her wealth in the midst of poverty, her hope where otherwise there was only despair.

Tears filled Krista's eyes. She thought of the times Jim had stepped between her and his father in the midst of a beating. When it was over and she had tenderly nursed her son's injuries, he would explain it away with the words of Saint Paul: "It is rare that anyone would lay down his life, even for a friend." Then he would add as he lay in his bed in that upstairs room: "But you are my mother."

When Jim looked up, he saw flies and mosquitoes buzzing around his mother. She seemed not to notice, but he did, and he felt sorry for her.

"Mom, the bugs are going to eat you alive. Why don't we move to the porch?" He went to her side and took her arm to help her up. Then he propped the hoe against the stool, and the two, arm in arm, slowly began to make their way out of the garden. They paused long enough for Jim to pick up the bag of medicine and place it in his pocket.

Continuing their walk, Jim steadied his mother until they reached the porch and made their way up the steps. They sat on old press-back chairs. Neither mentioned going inside where Ed sat in his rocker by a far window. They didn't want to risk the hell that waited within. His abuse was only verbal now, not physical, but heaped on the scars of the past it hurt with the same intensity.

Krista began reliving all of the memories that had kept her going. Jim divided his attention between the far-off woods and his mother. He smiled and touched her hand.

When she began to talk about the dog he had from fourth grade through high school, Jim was more attentive. His mother had given him the dog as a birthday present. It was black with tan markings on its face and a white tip on the tail. The shorthaired mixed breed had grown into a fair-sized dog. Jim called it Ranger. With a great deal of patience Jim taught the dog how to hunt pheasants. When he spoke of its merits to his peers, he said it was one of the finest hunting dogs one could have. It had been Jim's companion. The two were inseparable. "I loved Ranger," Jim said quietly.

"I know," his mother said. "I don't know how many times I watched you and that dog sit on this porch or go off into the woods to hunt. When you talked to him, it seemed as if he could understand. I know...."

"Dad shot Ranger," Jim said. "He shot him for no reason at all other than to get at me. It was the third of July. He laughed as he went back in the house. Said it was pre-holiday fireworks."

"You held Ranger on your lap the rest of the afternoon and into the night," Krista said. "You didn't come in for supper. You just sat there and cried until there weren't any tears left. I was afraid to come out and sit with you. Afraid of what Ed would do to me."

"I understood, Mom."

"I was already in bed when you finally buried Ranger."

Krista's eyes moved from Jim across the lawn to a place by the barn where a fieldstone marked the spot.

"It was the third of July," Jim said softly.

"I wouldn't have known how to comfort you if I could have," Krista said. "But I cried for you. I still didn't know what to say the next day. There wasn't anything I could think of that would have eased the pain. And if I had tried, Ed would have beaten me."

"Don't worry, Mom. We both understand." Jim studied the makeshift headstone by the barn. "That was what hurt so much. I could talk to Ranger even when there wasn't a chance to talk to you because of Dad. He shot the one companion that was always there to share things with."

"I'm sorry."

"Don't be sorry, Mom. It wasn't your fault. That's all in the past now. He can yell, but he can't hurt us."

They both sat, enjoying each other's company. The sun was beginning its arch into the west, shining right into their faces.

"I love you, Mom."

"Your love has given me reason to live," Krista answered. "Please be the son I have loved. I don't know what the doctors did or what medicine they gave you, but please take it."

"I will. Don't worry. That's all over. I know what I have to do. I want to be here to take care of you."

Jim squinted. The sun was directly in his eyes. A deer fly landed on his left wrist. Jim swatted it and it fell to the porch. He thought of how his dad made a practice of swatting the flies on his arm and then studying them in death before brushing them off on the floor. It was just another of those small aggravating habits that revealed his father's inner feelings toward those around him.

"I don't want to lose this moment any more than you do, but maybe we better go inside," Jim said to his mother.

They got up from their chairs. The screen door squeaked as Jim opened it and held it for his mother.

"Where the hell have you been?" Ed shouted at Krista, ignoring Jim. "When are we going to eat? I've been sitting here all day! Damned woman anyway!"

Krista hastened to the refrigerator to get out some food. She knew that only an immediate response would stop the yelling.

Having got his way with his wife, Ed turned his attention to Jim. "Well, look who's back! My good-for-nothing asshole son."

Jim didn't respond, instead moving to his dad's side. Looking over Ed's shoulder, he pointed out the window toward the hay field that lay between the yard and the woods. "Look, Dad, a doe and two fawns. Think there's a buck in the velvet getting ready to step out of the woods? They should be getting their horns by now."

Ed looked toward the woods. As he was studying the woods in silence, Krista set the table. When the cold supper was ready, Jim helped his father from his rocking chair to his place at the table.

"Tell me again about that northern pike you caught at Ennis Lake," Jim said to his father, hoping to create a diversion.

Ed speared a slice of beef roast and began to tell the story as if it was the first time.

"No one had fished on Ennis Lake for a long time. One summer I got the idea to try it. I went alone and found it was filled with big northern pike. They hadn't been fished in so long they had grown to be a pretty good size. Every night I would catch at least one. I'd always tell everybody I was fishing in Buffalo Lake by the railroad overpass. They never did catch on.

"Well, this one night I was fishing out of a boat with a cane pole, using a minnow for bait. The bobber disappeared with a splash and I knew it was a big one. When I set the hook, the fish jumped, and I knew it would weigh twenty pounds or more! If I had held on to the pole, it would have broke. I threw it overboard and let the fish drag it around the lake until it was exhausted. Then I rowed over and retrieved the pole and the fish. It was the biggest northern ever caught in this area."

After they had eaten, Jim helped his father shuffle back to his rocker. Jim sat on a threadbare sofa that was covered with a rag rug. In a practice that had once been familiar, he led Ed from one story to another, and the evening passed without incident.

When they had finished all the hunting, fishing, and

boxing stories, Jim excused himself. Taking a glass of water from the sink to use with his medicine, he said good night to his mother and climbed the steps to his bedroom.

The glow from the light in the hall helped him find the bare bulb hanging from its cord in the center of the bedroom ceiling. Jim pulled the cord and the forty-watt bulb cast a dull glow in the room. Then he set the water on the dresser and reached in his pocket for the medicine, which he placed beside it. He sat on the edge of his bed and studied the room for a long time. The wallpaper had turned brown, and the colors in its decorative flowers had faded. Corners of it had begun to pull from the wall, revealing the plaster behind it.

There were three pieces of furniture in the room: A dark wooden dresser, the iron bed he was sitting on and his gun cabinet. A curtain rod had been stretched across the top of the cabinet and an old piece of red cloth covered his guns.

Jim got up from the bed and walked over to the cabinet. He pushed the cloth to one side and stared at the guns. They were just as he had left them. He took out the .223 Savage that had been his deer rifle. There were spots of rust on it. He would have to get the oil out and polish it in the morning. Just holding it brought back memories of his successful hunts. He brought it to his shoulder and took sight at an imaginary deer in the wallpaper. Then he put it back in its place. The other guns were still there – his .22, twelve-gauge shotgun, and his father's Browning automatic. As he looked down toward where the stocks rested on the shelf, he noticed three twelve-gauge slugs standing on their brass ends near the Browning automatic. Jim smiled and thought back to a different era. One always had to be ready in case a buck stepped out in that hay field and offered itself as meat for the month. The plugs were usually in the guns shell chambers so they would be legal for duck hunting. Three shells were all either would hold.

Jim pulled the curtain on the gun cabinet shut, then

sat down on the bed. The guns needed cleaning and oiling. Then he looked at the glass of water and medicine on the dresser. Dark memories of his father began to flood his mind, and the drab bedroom made it worse. Depression set in. He knew that there would be no escape, no more highs. He needed those highs. God, he needed those highs.

The only other items in the bedroom were a crucifix and a calendar hanging on the wall, and three sets of antlers, including Jim's favorite eight-pointer. Jim's eyes shifted from the medicine to the crucifix. Christ had spent three days in the tomb. Lazarus had spent three days in the tomb. He had been in the hospital three days and now he had come back from the dead. Or was he still dead? If he didn't take the medicine, would he rise from the dead and burst forth from the tomb like Lazarus and Jesus?

He looked at the place on the dresser where he always put his Bible. Then he remembered. He had left it in the rack on the back of a pew in front of the Elijah window in St. Bridget's. He would have to go get it, but not right away. He wanted to stay away from Wisconsin Dells for a while. Besides, tomorrow he planned to take his mother to Portage. He hadn't taken her for a ride in a long time, and he knew she would enjoy it.

16

Jim sat on the edge of his bed. He couldn't remember how many days had gone by. The medicine was still on the dresser. He was in a state of euphoria. Elijah had returned in all his splendor. Devils darted among the flowers in the wallpaper. There was nothing to fear. An angel hovered protectively over him in the glow of the light. Michael the Archangel stood ready to defend the new Elijah.

He had risen from the hospital tomb of three days. The doctors had tried to poison him with their medicine, destroy his mind with their talk. The exhilaration of risen life coursed through his veins. Jim looked at the crucifix and understood why everyone worshipped Christ. They envied Him for something so few had ever felt. But Jim had. He, too, had broken the bonds of death. He had left behind the white shrouds of the hospital. The locked doors of its special ward could not contain him.

Jim's eyes, flashing in the milieu of resurrected life, darted about the room and momentarily came to rest on the calendar. He knew it was Friday. What was the date? It had to be Friday, the third of July. There was a message there, but what was it?

Unable to contain himself, Jim jumped from the bed and made his way down the stairs. He pushed open the white, four-panel door with its porcelain knob. As he walked into the kitchen, he found his mother in despair.

"Please, Jim, have you taken your pills? You just don't understand, do you?" she pleaded. Her eyes filled with tears as she shuffled into the downstairs bedroom and closed the door.

Jim looked at his father who lifted his coffee can from the floor and spat a brown spray of tobacco into it. Ed put the can down and rocked for a moment, then took a fly swatter from its place on the windowsill. A fly moved along the wall within his reach. He hit it, held it against the wall for a moment, then let it drop to the floor.

July third. His dad. Ranger.

"Kill!" the Voice demanded.

Jim stood, confused. He looked past his father and into the woods. The Devil darted among the trees.

"You are Elijah. You have come to rid the world of its false priests. Kill."

But whom? The command of the Voice resonated throughout his body. He needed direction. And then, with the impact of a twenty-pound stone thrown from a cliff into a creek it came to him. His Bible. The message had to be in the Bible and the window. Elijah would speak to him!

Without a word he burst through the screen door and ran to his car. He started it, threw the transmission in reverse, then backed out on the driveway. As he stopped before turning on the road, he glanced at the small red sign with the farm's fire number. It was a number that caught his attention: 333...July third...333.

He entered Wisconsin Dells on Highway 23. It was obvious that the biggest week of the tourist season had arrived. No Vacancy signs were everywhere. People crowded the sidewalks and filled the crosswalks. The more daring jaywalked between cars that were snarled on Broadway.

Eventually Jim reached the railroad trestle that passed over the street at the west end of the old business district. He waited for what seemed an eternity for an opening in traffic so he could cross and enter the parking lot. It was the main place to park for the Upper Dells boat trip. Finding the right parking space was difficult, but Jim was sure his car would go unnoticed. It was obscured by the railroad embankment on one side and the Wisconsin River on the other. By walking out the south end and over the railroad tracks, he would be only one block from St. Bridget's.

Jim quickly crossed the lot. Within minutes he was on LaCrosse Street and invisible in the crowd. He walked south and at the intersection took Washington Avenue past Zinke's Grocery store. St. Bridget's School was separated from the store by an alley that ran parallel to Washington Avenue.

Jim stopped at the corner of Washington and Oak Street. He glanced down Oak Street at the police station and noticed no squad cars were parked in front. Chief Iverson and his two deputies were occupied with the onslaught of tourists. Jim looked in the opposite direction at St. Bridget's. He could not hear a lawn mower nor see Duke working in front of the church. The blinds were drawn in Fr. Ross' office.

It was a risk, but one he had to take. He needed the direction that only his Bible and some time in front of the window of Elijah could give. Only then would he know what he was supposed to do. Elijah would take him into the end time.

Jim walked down Washington Street toward Nickolai Funeral Home. Just before he reached it, he crossed the street and cut between two houses and the parking lot on the north side of the church. The handicap ramp was on the north side of the church and, with any luck, the door would be open. It opened into the baptismal area. The window of Elijah was above it. One could sit in that alcove without being immediately noticed by someone coming in through the main entrance. There was a risk that someone could come out through the sacristy door in the sanctuary opposite the north alcove, but if there was no one in the sacristy already, one would hear steps on the metal stairway and the outside door open.

Jim studied the interior of the church through the plate glass door of the handicap ramp. There were no lights inside except the light of the late morning sun shining through the stained-glass windows of the sanctuary. Jim waited. No one was moving about inside the church. He pressed the button and the door swung open. He watched while the door stayed open its designated time. No one came to see who was entering.

Jim stepped into the cool darkness of the church. He looked again to make sure no one was in the church. He walked down the side aisle to where he remembered being on his previous visit. As he walked, he looked at the back of each pew and the rack that held hymnals and missalettes. Finally he saw his black leather Bible with gold-edged pages standing on end in one of the racks. He entered the pew and sat down. He looked up and saw the sun shining through the Elijah glass with a brilliance he had never seen. The colors rained down on him with a power he had never felt. Jim was awestruck.

He pulled the Bible from the rack and it fell open to the first book of Kings and the unfaithful Jeroboam who offered sacrifices upon the altar to the golden calf idol at Bethel. Then, at the Lord's command, the prophet shouted, "O altar...a child to be born shall sacrifice upon you the priests of the shrines on the hills who come here to burn incense; and men's bones shall be burned upon you."

The words before his eyes filled every corner of his mind. "Child to be born...Child to be born...! Priests... Men's bones to be burned." Over and over the words reverberated in his mind until they took on a life of their own.

Jim looked up and was blinded by color. The arm of Elijah moved above him in blessing and anointing. The fierce eyes stared into the very core of Jim's being, igniting his soul with a passion he had never felt before. Slowly the thin cheeks of Elijah drew inward as words began to take form. The words of Elijah rocked the very foundation of St. Bridget's. "You are the bearer of my cloak. My power rests upon you!"

The sanctuary candle flickered and began to rise in intensity. Soon it burst its upward bounds and became the Devil incarnate. Elijah thrust his arm in the direction of Jim and shouted, "You have my power! You are the New Elijah! You must destroy Evil and its false priests."

As if rising from a baptismal font, Jim stood and raised both hands above his head. He waved his Bible in confirmation and shouted in return, "Yes!"

Suddenly a cloud covered the sun and the window returned to normal, but the Devil remained, slowly dancing down the opposite side of the church and across the back until he reached the confessional. He turned to Jim and smiled like a veteran warrior who was seldom defeated. Then he pulled open the door where the priest sat and disappeared within.

How many times had Jim entered one of those side doors and asked that the devil be removed from his life? How many times had the priest failed to do so? He had come here as a child. He had come here as an adult.

Fr. Ross had not helped. Now he understood why. The priest within that confessional was a false priest who burned incense to the golden calf idol. Elijah had stood up to 450 false prophets. He, the New Elijah, was ordained to bring one more to sacrifice. Fr. Ross' bones must be burned upon an altar.

The vision disappeared when Jim heard the outside sacristy door open. He jumped up from the pew and fled through the handicap door. Leaping the iron rail, he ran between the houses and was soon back on Washington Street, moving through the crowd in the direction of his car.

Duke walked through the sacristy, paused in the sanctuary to look through the patio doors that formed the entrance to the cry room opposite the sacristy, and then slowly made his way to the main aisle of the church. As he walked he looked up at the choir loft. He pushed through the double doors leading to the vestibule, opened one of the main plate glass doors and walked out onto the upper level of the entrance. As he did, he noticed Fr. Ross coming out of the rectory and turned to meet him on the sidewalk in front of the Blessed Virgin Shrine.

"I was just coming back from the cemetery to eat lunch in the basement of the church, and I would swear I heard a voice," Duke said. "But I walked through the church and didn't see anyone." As he was talking, he reached in his shirt pocket, took out a pack of Salems and a book of matches, shook a cigarette loose and put the pack back in his pocket. He lit a cigarette, inhaled the huge first drag from it and spoke again.

"Have you heard anything about Jim Elliot?"

"I called the hospital a couple of days after Dan took him over there but they won't say anything about him, claiming confidentiality. I suppose I could go over there, but first there was the weekend and now the Fourth of July to contend with. I can't believe we wouldn't have seen him by now if he was home again. Have to say it's been peaceful without him."

"If he does return, I can tell you one person who isn't going to put up with him," said Duke, pausing for emphasis. He took another puff on his cigarette, then continued. "Dan Iverson is just waiting to slap a felony charge on him.

"One of his deputies stopped in the cemetery to ask if I had seen him. He told me that after Dan got Jim loaded in the back seat and ready to take to Oshkosh, he stopped at the police station and left Jim locked in the back of the car while he ran in to get something. He hadn't put handcuffs on Jim, and in the few moments Dan was gone, Jim pissed through the grill separating the front and back seats. He soaked the seats, the console, the radio, the mobile data computer, and all the papers in a briefcase Dan had left open on the front passenger seat.

"According to the deputy, Dan was in a hurry and didn't notice what Jim had done until he sat down in a puddle in his vinyl bucket seat. He was ready to kill Jim when he pulled him from the car and put him in another car to make the trip to Oshkosh. It cost a hundred bucks to get the car cleaned, and they still don't know if the radio and computer can be fixed.

"The worst part came when Dan went home. You know how his wife has a fit about being neat and clean. The deputy says she made him leave the uniform in the garage. She wasn't about to touch it or have it in the house.

"The deputies have been having a lot of fun teasing Dan. They keep asking what Jim did that caused him to pee in his own pants."

"Guess I fail to see anything funny about a guy who wants to have you rise in the nude from behind an altar," Fr. Ross interjected. After an awkward silence Fr. Ross continued, "Not to change the subject, but how does the cemetery look? And don't forget, the church has to be dusted!"

"I know." Duke turned and made his escape toward the church.

Back at his car, Jim sat quietly. He had all afternoon

to make a plan and get ready. After reading his Bible for an hour, he started his car and drove to St. Bridget's cemetery, which was located on a hill on the north side of town. He made his way back up Broadway, turned left onto Church Street, and turned right on Indiana Avenue, which borders the cemetery. As he drove past the cemetery, he noticed Duke mowing. His back was toward Jim. Jim couldn't stop or go in the cemetery, but didn't have to. What he needed was standing halfway up the hill surrounded by tall bushes – a white altar with a large crucifix behind it and two figures kneeling on either side of the crucifix.

Jim drove back to Broadway, turned left, and took Highway 23 toward his parents' house. When he reached the driveway, he looked at the fire number 333, but did not turn in. Instead, he drove to the next intersection, Grotzke Road, and turned left. A mile down it he found what he was looking for. An abandoned farmhouse stood in the trees and weeds beside the road. As a child he had led classmates there, telling them it was haunted. It was not the house that attracted him now. It was the desolate woods behind it.

He followed the grass-covered road to its destination at the base of a steep hill. The area was frequented by deer hunters in the fall, but he knew he would be alone there in the middle of summer. He parked the car and hiked to the top, then walked to the rocky cliff that formed the northern edge. It had been a favorite place during his childhood. Pretending to be a mountain climber, he had scaled its three-hundred-foot-high cliff more than once. His most vivid memory was of a spring afternoon when he had brought three schoolmates here to show them how to climb it. That afternoon, showing off, he had chosen a more treacherous path to the top than usual. As he neared the top, his foot had slipped, and only the small tree he grabbed in desperation had saved him.

Now he sat at the top looking down at the rocks that had broken loose and lay at the base of the cliff. Beyond it, through the trees, curled the Neenah Creek. In the distance, at least a mile away, was the farmhouse where his parents lived. This had always been his refuge. It was the place he and his dog, Ranger, had come when life became unbearable. He thought of the story of Elijah and how, after the king had put the 450 false prophets to death, Jezebel had called out the armies to kill him. Elijah had hidden in a cave until the voice of God came in the form of the gentle breeze. Jim could feel the gentle breeze now. It was the same breeze that carried away flies and mosquitoes that threatened to eat anyone out there alive. It was that breeze in which Jim heard the Voice telling him what he must do.

Jim rose and made his way back to the car. He opened the trunk of the Chevrolet and checked the supplies he would need. During his travels the trunk of his car had become his home. It held his few clothes, some bottled water and canned food, metal eating and cooking utensils, rope, duct tape and matches. He also kept, among other things, a machete, various knives, and a .357 police revolver with a two-inch barrel in the trunk.

Jim took out the roll of tape, several pieces of rope, the matches, and a twenty-ounce Coke bottle of gas for starting fires. He placed them on the front seat, then returned to the trunk, unzipped a cloth case and removed the revolver from it. He flipped open the cylinder, reached back in the trunk and grabbed a box of bullets. Then he loaded the revolver, slipped it beneath his belt and pulled his T-shirt over it. It was compact, but if someone looked closely, he would see it. Where he was going there would be no one to look. Besides, darkness would be his friend. He slammed the trunk lid closed and began the final part of his preparation; filling the back seat and passenger seat with dry wood from fallen trees. Then Jim began his drive back into Wisconsin Dells. He knew by the position of the sun that Duke had left the cemetery for the day.

As expected, the cemetery was vacant when Jim arrived. He entered through the gate and followed the

road that led to the altar. He wanted to unload his supplies quickly, using the cover of the bushes, and then
drive the car out of the cemetery and hide it. There
was only the one entrance to the cemetery, and it would
be easy to get trapped inside with a car.

Jim stacked everything between the bushes and the
altar. Even if someone came by, his materials would go
unnoticed. Then he got back in his car and drove out
of the cemetery. The east and north sides of the cemetery were bordered by a stand of trees that were part
of Camp Waubeek. It was a camp used primarily for
school children, and it was vacant this time of the year.
Jim drove back to Broadway, turned east, and traveled
up Highway 16 to the entrance of the camp.

A cable stretched between two posts blocked the
entrance. A padlock secured one end, but a previous
visitor had neglected to snap the lock shut. Jim noticed
it immediately and was soon within the campgrounds.
He took a road leading to the back side of the cemetery.
He found a pavilion that was simply a roof supported
by posts, and drove his car up on the concrete slab.

From above, his car would go unnoticed.

After securing the vehicle, he made his way over the
crest of the hill and back into the cemetery. Most people
didn't understand, he thought to himself. Being a soldier was hard work. Being a soldier of God was even
more difficult. He laid the wood he had brought in the
car on the altar and went back into the woods to get
more. Jim was sweating by the time he finished the
project. He took a sharp-pointed piece of wood and
scraped a crude ditch around the altar. Doing the will
of God was exacting and demanding. If he was going to
be the new Elijah, he had to surpass the old Elijah.

He sat down in the shade and security of the bushes
to rest awhile before making the final preparations.
Then Jim untied his bundles of rope and laid some long
pieces along the back side of the altar, placing the gasoline and matches beside them. Before leaving the camp-
ground he had found two five-gallon cans of gas out-

side a utility shed. He brought them with him. He would pour the contents of the cans into the trench around the altar at the appropriate time. He had laid his revolver on the ground while he carried wood. He retrieved it, placed it in his belt, and sat down to conceive a plan for getting Fr. Ross to the cemetery.

July third. It was a holy day. There were three persons in the Trinity. Jesus was thirty-three when he died. He had been born on July third. As with the people of the Exodus, his house had been marked with a special sign — 333. But sin had entered into this holiest of days. His father had shot Ranger. Shot Ranger and taunted him as only the devil could. The day must be purged and made holy once again.

The prophetic arm of Elijah raised itself before him and he listened to the Voice. "Kill! You are the only one who has the power! Purify the earth."

The feeling of power filled Jim's body, blocking out any fear he had. A true soldier had to overcome fear. The Voice steeled his will. "Kill." He could see the devil darting about in the trees at the edge of the cemetery. Then Jim saw something else. At first he thought it was an illusion. Then he realized it was real. God and Elijah were working with him. Fr. Ross' Fiero had just driven through the entrance to the cemetery. He must have decided to check Duke's work to see if everything was ready for the weekend. Jim dove behind the altar before Fr. Ross saw him.

From his hiding place Jim watched as Fr. Ross slowly drove up the hill. Fr. Ross stopped. No doubt he had noticed the altar with the wood stacked on it. Jim watched as Fr. Ross swung the door of the car open and worked his way out of the low-slung vehicle. The door squeaked as he closed it. Fr. Ross took a few steps toward the altar. *He has to be wondering why Duke left such a mess,* Jim thought to himself. He panicked for a moment and then realized that was not befitting of a true prophet. He was in charge. He was in command of the happenings upon this earth. Elijah had given him the power of life and death.

Without realizing what he was doing, Jim found himself standing, face to face with Fr. Ross.

"Jim. What are you doing here?" Fr. Ross hadn't expected to find anyone here, least of all Jim. What was he doing by the altar? What was this mess? Had Jim created it? Fr. Ross couldn't believe Duke would leave something like this for the Fourth of July weekend, it was almost an act of desecration.

"Jim, what are you doing here? I thought you were in the hospital."

"Oh, I was for three days! I have risen from the dead. You sent me there. I wouldn't let them fry my brain! Besides, Fr. Claude said there is nothing wrong with me."

"Jim, you need to go back to the hospital."

"No. The doctors didn't find anything wrong with me. They told me they wished everyone was as crazy as me. They tried to force medicine into me. Poison! I took it only long enough to satisfy them. I knew what they wanted to do."

"Jim, you have to go back to the hospital."

"No, Fr. Claude said that if you filled out any papers trying to keep me there, they should be torn up."

Rage was building in Jim's voice. The young man had moved very close, and Fr. Ross could feel his breath on his face. He was about to step back when Jim hooked a leg behind his and hit him in the chest with his forearm.

Fr. Ross tumbled backward and fell on the ground. Jim rolled him over and pinned an arm behind his back. The pain was ripping through that arm when he felt his other wrist being brought up behind him. The pain in his arms was surpassed only by the pain in his back, caused by Jim ramming his knee into it and knocking the wind from his lungs. In the haze he could feel a rope drawing his wrists together.

Jim eased away from him slowly. Still on his hands and knees, he bowed his head toward Fr. Ross' upturned ear and whispered, "I am the new Elijah!"

Now Jim kicked Fr. Ross in the ribs. His father had kicked Ranger. A false priest deserved the same. When he had exacted his vengeance, Jim grabbed Fr. Ross and dragged him behind the altar. He tied his feet, then rested. It was not dark yet. It must be the wishes of Elijah that the fire be built during the day. Then he remembered that the false priests had prayed all morning, and Elijah had taken over at noon.

From his vantage point near the top of the hill Jim looked to see if anyone else was in the cemetery, which was unlikely. It had to be supper time. If people weren't eating, they were working or preparing for the weekend.

Satisfied that they were alone, Jim reached down and lifted Fr. Ross' semiconscious body. He put him on the altar. Bracing him with his own shoulder, Jim brought Fr. Ross' legs and feet up to the altar. He rolled Fr. Ross over on his back and looped the longer pieces of rope that he had placed behind the altar over his body and under the ends of the altar table. He drew the ropes tight and tied them.

Then Jim took the bottle of gas that he had brought with him and splashed it on the wood beneath Fr. Ross. He took the five-gallon cans, turned the covers off the spouts, and dumped the contents in the trench around the altar. When he was done, he threw both the bottle and the cans in the bushes.

As Jim worked feverishly, Fr. Ross began to regain his senses. He smelled the gas and felt the sharp ends of the sticks piercing his back. Fear flooded his mind. He knew he had to control himself or he would never escape. He had to think of something to say, but there wasn't anything he could say. He was at the mercy of insanity.

Looking at Jim's face, all he could think of was a Halloween mask. It was meant to scare, and it did. But the purpose of Halloween was to give people the opportunity to face their fears and overcome them.

Fr. Ross thought of his own impending death and of

one of the most introspective sermons he had ever given. Perhaps it wasn't the worst thing in the world to die young. He had witnessed cancer and seen its torturous death played out a hundred times. That was the death he feared most. But what if he was to accept cancer's presence in his body? To know the pain that was going to be there and yet tell doctors not to administer any drugs to relieve it. Face the pain head on and offer it up for his sins and the lives of the people he knew. As he strained against the ropes, he knew cancer was not the immediate threat.

Fr. Ross turned his face as far as he could and looked directly at Jim. How many Elijahs had there been in his life? Had he ever done anything that helped them? Nothing. He felt so empty, so worthless, and now he knew he must pay. He wanted to say he forgave Jim. Jim's eyes seemed to burn right through to the back of his head. Fr. Ross dropped his returning stare and tried to gather the strength to forgive.

"When two dogs fight, the first to drop its stare is the loser," Jim whispered. "You are a loser, but we knew that. I am Elijah, the Master of life and death at the moment. I came to you and asked you to drive the devil from me. You were not able to exorcise him. Therefore, you are a false prophet and must be put to death.

"Are you afraid of what is going to happen, false prophet? You should be, because I am going to send you to hell. That is the difference between us. When you die, your deeds will be rewarded with unquenchable fire. Should I die, I will go straight to heaven for I am God's chosen one. I have no fear, for my deeds will take me to heaven."

Taking a wooden kitchen match from a box, Jim scraped it across the stone altar. Fr. Ross saw the tip burst into flame. It was as if every detail was suspended in time, lasting an eternity. Jim held the match between two fingers as he shielded the flame with his other hand. The words that he screamed as an incantation were impossible to understand – loud, filled with hate and rage. He dropped the match in the ditch and jumped back. The fire started slowly at first and then made its way around the altar. Before it had returned to its starting place the flames blocked Jim's vision of Fr. Ross. The wood caught fire. Jim waited for the scream within the fire – the sign that he had conquered.

"What the hell is going on?" Duke's voice resounded through the cemetery like a clap of thunder.

Jim started running.

Duke ran toward the altar. Without thinking of his own safety he jumped through the outer wall of flame. What he thought he saw as he entered the cemetery was true. Fr. Ross was tied to the altar. In a reflex motion he pulled his jackknife out of his pocket and cut the ropes binding Fr. Ross' legs, then slashed the ropes across his chest. The wood was blazing and Fr. Ross' clothes were on fire.

Duke grabbed Fr. Ross and pulled him through the circle of flames. He was still rolling him on the grass, trying to extinguish his flaming clothes when Dan Iverson drove up.

"What's going on? You can see the smoke and flames all over town!" Iverson yelled as he ran toward the two figures on the grass.

"It was Jim Elliot!" Duke shouted, straightening up for a moment. "The son of a bitch went that way." Duke pointed toward the main part of town. He continued rolling Fr. Ross on the grass.

Iverson pulled his radio from his belt, summoned an ambulance, and then alerted his deputies. He jumped in his squad car and headed back to Broadway and the downtown area.

Jim vaulted the fence on the west side of the cemetery near an old water tower. He was disoriented and running blindly. How could anyone stand in the way of Elijah's plan?

An aimless, five-block run/walk took him into the wooded area behind the houses along Indiana Avenue and River Road, then to Broadway, which was filled with people. Neon lights were flashing everywhere, but they weren't just lights. They were the devil's contortions screaming out at him, taunting him. He put his hands over his ears and closed his eyes. He was a failure as a prophet. As with the original Elijah, Jezebel's army was in full pursuit.

He opened his eyes to see lights approaching, those of a squad car flashing blue and red on the bridge over the Wisconsin River. He must escape, but the entrance to the parking lot was blocked.

Jim looked to his right. There was a metal railing and a gate that served as the off-ramp for the Upper Dells boat ride. He could see the boats moored on the river below. He jumped the railing, landing on the sidewalk, then leaped a wooden fence, ran through a strip of grass and dropped down on the next sidewalk. Jim hopped over another wooden fence into a flower bed on the level of the docks.

As he ran past a startled guard at the exit booth, he noticed the *Queen of the Dells* was departing for its evening cruise up the Wisconsin River to the Indian Ceremonial at Stand Rock. The thirty-six-ton, fifty-four-foot metal boat was outfitted with rows of lawn chairs on its upper deck and rows of lawn chairs behind three rows of heavy wooden seats below. It held 125 passengers and it was full.

The guide was beginning her opening remarks as Jim jumped from the dock to the back deck of the boat. Pulling his revolver from his belt, he ran up the aisle between the lawn chairs. Maddened by the devil's taunts and the sight of the squad car, he struck the pilot, who was maneuvering the boat away from the dock. The pilot slumped forward over the steering wheel. Jim grabbed him by the shirt and threw him out of his chair.

He waved the gun as a warning to the guide and looked back at the crowd, but the crowd had disappeared. The devil was there in legions. Jim fired one shot and the .357 bullet ricocheted off the metal ceiling, striking a woman in the shoulder. She screamed, but for Jim it was Legion screaming.

When he was a senior in high school Jim had worked on the boats during the summer. In the confusion of the moment, he strained to remember how to operate the boat. On the upper right of the console, to the left of all the gauges, were two black-knobbed shift levers mounted close enough together to be operated with one hand. They had been pulled to the front of the console as the *Queen of the Dells* backed out into the main channel. Below the shift levers were two red-knobbed throttle levers. If he could operate a cabin cruiser on Lake Michigan, he could operate this boat.

Jim tucked his gun under his belt, grabbed the wheel, and pulled the throttle levers toward him. The two 318 Chrysler Marine engines roared in their compartments at the back half of the boat. An experienced pilot would have feathered the controls and found little need to use the wheel. Jim spun the handles of the wheel this way and that, and the boat cleared the dock. Then he jammed the shift levers from reverse, through neutral, and into forward. The throttles were wide open; he had almost torn the transmissions apart.

There were twelve gates in the dam below. When the power company opened eight, the boats were moved farther upstream for the boarding of passengers as the river current and its eddy became too strong to maneuver in. On this evening seven gates were already open and the power company was considering opening the eighth and ninth to control the high waters and swift current.

Frantically, Jim turned the wheel. He could see the high, limestone banks of the Wisconsin River towering over him on either side of the boat as it began to pick up speed.

The arm of Satan closed around his neck. Jim let go of the wheel to meet his adversary. He jammed an elbow into his opponent's rib cage and swung out from under the arm. Then he reached for his revolver and fired point blank into the man's chest. The would-be rescuer flew back over the body of the unconscious pilot into the aisle.

"I am the new Elijah!" Jim screamed as he turned back to the wheel and tried to grab its spinning wood knobs with his free hand. The knobs pounded his knuckles. Finally, he pushed his hip against the wheel and gained control. It was only then that he realized his mistake. As he looked out over the taunting forces of Legion behind him, he saw the concrete pillar that supported the railroad trestle. He looked up to see the trestle above and behind him. They had gone under it and were headed, full speed, toward the dam that held the waters of the Upper Dells.

Built in 1909 by the Wisconsin Power and Light Company, the dam stretched across the last of the high rock banks of the Wisconsin River in the area, separating what had become known as the upper Dells from the lower Dells. A white cement power station with large windows had been built on the east side of the river. A concrete base had been poured across the rest of the river. From it rose cement partitions that supported heavy metal gates that, in turn, raised the river a total of twenty feet.

Having gone under the old trestle, the *Queen of the Dells* traveled beneath the four-lane bridge that had been built to carry traffic back and forth between the two sections of the city. The prow of the boat was splitting the dark, tamarack-colored water at full speed with the aid of the strong current. White water churned behind the boat.

When the *Queen of the Dells* hit the gate, the passengers and lawn chairs flew forward with such force that those on the upper deck were thrown over the front railing into the waters immediately in front of the boat or over the dam. Those on the lower deck were propelled forward against the front of the boat. Jim was pinned against the wheel by passengers and seats that were sliding violently forward.

The metal gate buckled beneath the weight of the

boat. Shards of steel tore at the quarter-inch steel hull of the *Queen of the Dells*, penetrating the hull and tearing open the eighty-gallon fuel tanks that had been filled to capacity for the trip up river. The boat balanced on the remaining section of the gate for a moment, and then the weight of its passengers tilted it forward over the dam. It slid down the dam, landed on the prow, and then pitched forward into the lower Dells waters upside down. Before it sank, it burst into flames. As the fuel came to the surface of the water, the whole area was enveloped in flames.

Mike Weber and two other EMTs had responded to a call at the Lighthouse, a restaurant at the entrance to the docks. When Mike first heard screams he thought they were coming from the rides at nearby Riverview Park. Then he heard the scraping sound of metal against metal, coming from the area of the dam. He saw the bodies first, some landing on the concrete base of the dam, others in the water. Then he saw the boat, crashing over the dam. Passengers flew everywhere. Then came the fire. He watched in horror as it made its way up the dam and reached out on the waters below to catch those trying to swim to safety. He heard tortured screams everywhere. The pent-up waters came roaring through the broken gate, pushing an island of flame down river. Beneath him, in the swell, the boats began to strain at their moorings.

For Mike, the gates of hell had opened before him. He closed his eyes to block out the devastation, but then the humanitarian interests that had drawn him to be an EMT took over.

17

Duke brought Fr. Ross back from the Baraboo Hospital, and the two, along with Dan Iverson, were sitting in Fr. Ross' office.

"It will be days before we find all the bodies," Iverson said. "Some were crushed between the boat and the dam. Others were burned beyond recognition. Still others were carried underwater far down stream. Divers are searching some of the deeper sections of the river, like the 90-foot waters below Hawks Beak. Only eight people survived."

"What about Jim?" asked Fr. Ross. He made a motion as if to comb the hair on the side of his head, but it had been singed off in the fire.

As they were talking Fr. Ross glanced at a postcard from the Diocesan Office that lay on top of a stack of mail. It was a standard form announcing the death of a priest or a priest's parent. He had received them weekly through his priesthood. The words were always the same, "It is my sad duty to inform you of the death of...." That card could have been the one announcing his death. He was having a hard time reconciling his survival with so many deaths. Why hadn't God taken him, too?

"Jim is presumed dead," Iverson continued. "Divers found his shirt twisted around the steering wheel. We don't have a body, but at this point probably couldn't tell if we did. Some have disappeared forever, ground to nothing between the boat and the dam or the concrete below the dam. I called on his mother to tell her what had happened. He hasn't appeared at the farm. Reporters have been out there. Krista refuses to talk with them. Ed is swearing at everybody he comes in contact with and trying to run them all off."

Duke flipped a Salem from the cigarette pack in his hand. He watched Fr. Ross scowl and saw it as a sign he was returning to good health. Even though his routine check of the cemetery before heading home from work had saved Fr. Ross' life, Duke knew he wouldn't be offered an ashtray and would have to hold the ashes in his hand or place them in the cuff of his overalls. Fr. Ross hated smoking in his office. As Duke lit the cigarette, he turned to Dan.

"You and the hospital in Oshkosh could have prevented all this." Duke let the sentence hang as a judgment.

Iverson ignored the comment. Given the circumstances, how would he ever explain to Duke the fine points of the law? The law states that one has to be a threat to himself or others. The law also states that a hospital cannot reveal whether it is holding a person for psychological evaluation. Telling someone he is going to rise from the dead from behind an altar or pissing all over a car seat didn't seem that serious to the doctor the day he had taken Jim to Oshkosh. In fact, the doctor had laughed. He might have, too, had he been the doctor. He had thought Fr. Ross' story amusing when he first heard it.

"We've connected Jim with the murder of a priest at St. Peter's in Skokie, Illinois," said Iverson, hoping to change the subject. "The description of it fits with what happened to Fr. Ross. Cemetery, altar... the whole bit. It's developing into a national story."

The phone rang. Krista wasn't the only one being hounded by reporters. Fr. Ross' office had been swamped with calls from the media, requesting interviews. There was no doubt in his mind that it was a story of national proportions. Fr. Ross hesitated until the third ring and then reached for the phone. Pain shot through his bruised ribs as he lifted his arm.

"St. Bridget's, Fr. Ross."

"F..a..thur."

Fr. Ross turned his head toward Duke and rolled his eyes. He knew that Duke was close enough to hear the conversation.

"Rose."

"F..a..thur. I have something important to tell you about my personal life."

"Rose, do you think it could wait? I have Duke and Police Chief Iverson with me, and we are discussing the loss of life when the boat went over the dam."

"F..a..thur. This is about my personal life."

"I still am trying to get over an attempt on my life. Could it wait?"

"You never want to listen to me. Remember my third husband? He never had a job."

"Yes, Rose, I remember you calling the recliner he always sat in the unemployment chair."

"That's the one. He wore that recliner out. Well, he had a favorite tree out in the front yard that died this spring. A neighbor asked if I wanted it cut down. While he was sawing it up, I dragged the chair out in the back yard, and we stacked the tree on top of it. I burned his tree and his chair. I am free of any memory of him. Can I come and talk about it?"

"No," Fr. Ross said. "No, Rose. I don't want to talk about fire for a long time. Not with you or anybody else."

18

The water's current carried Jim to the sandy shore of the river, just south of the power station. Across the river and up stream he could see the flashing lights of the rescue vehicles. His shirt and one of his shoes were lost, his jeans and socks were soaked, and he was covered with sand. Though weak, he knew he had to flee the area. Jezebel would certainly have her armies after him and would chase him to the edge of the desert and beyond.

He was a failure as the new Elijah, and yet he felt a sense of exhilaration. He had almost killed the false priest. No pill or drug, legal or illegal, could give him the same sensation. He couldn't understand how he had failed. Where had Duke come from anyway?

Jim climbed through the brush along the shore, crossed the railroad tracks, and came out in the city behind the baseball diamond and swimming pool. Across a large parking lot he could see St. Bridget's. Cars were parked in front and all the lights in the rectory were on. Was Fr. Ross there? He saw television vans and press vehicles all around. Reporters and parishioners were milling about on the front sidewalk. He needed an explanation and a new sense of direction, but a visit to Elijah was out of the question.

Jim circled around behind the baseball diamond seeking the shelter of the woods that surrounded it. He moved from shadow to shadow, house to house, along Bowman Street until he came to the City Park. He crossed it and crouched in the safety of the bushes until there was a lull in the traffic. As he looked downtown, one of the neon signs caught his attention. Something was wrong! It gave the time: 11:00 p.m. It gave the temperature: 82 degrees, and the date: Wednesday, July 1st. How could that be? Having looked at the calendar that very morning, he knew that it was Friday, July 3rd.

Mesmerized, Jim watched the sign go through its cycle a number of times. Each time it said Wednesday, July 1st. Then he looked at still another sign advertising the next scheduled boat trips. It said Thursday, July 2nd. What had happened? Slowly he began to realize the trick the devils in his bedroom wallpaper had played on him. The calendar on the wall was one that had been hanging there since before his long sojourn. Today was indeed Friday, July 3rd – years ago. The devils had tricked him just like they did when they changed the traffic lights. They had wanted to see him die, had even gone so far as to plan his destruction on that boat. No wonder he had failed. This was not the appointed day for the return of Elijah!

Staying hidden as much as possible, Jim made his way past Van Wie's Dells Lumber Yard and through the gate of the cemetery. As he walked past the altar, he looked up at the crucified figure of Christ towering over it. In the moonlight he could see that the white, cement statue had been blackened. The Lord must certainly be angry with him for being led astray by the devil. He had to get into hiding and think of a way to make amends.

Mosquitoes attacked him throughout his trek back to the car. The foot without a shoe was swollen, and his chest ached. He opened the trunk of his car and took out some fresh clothes. He put on a clean T-shirt and jeans. The wet jeans and underwear went into the trunk. He threw the shoe that had remained on his foot into the bushes near the pavilion. With some difficulty he put on dry running shoes. Then he closed the trunk and got into the driver's seat.

Jim took the back roads from the Dells to the farm where his parents lived. He drove past their driveway and turned left on Grotzke Road. When he got to the drive by the haunted house, he cut off the headlights and trusted moonlight to guide him back to the bluff and his hiding spot. Stopping the car, he opened the trunk and took out some bug spray and a sleeping bag. There was a cave among the rocks near the crest of the hill. He had found it as a youth and had never told anyone. It was where he and Ranger came when they were seeking safety from home. Now he would use it to hide from Jezebel's army. This was the cave on the side of Mount Horeb where Elijah had eaten and slept and gained strength to carry out the Lord's command.

Jim slept most of Thursday. He left the cave one time to get some canned food from the trunk of his car and water from the Neenah Creek. He brought back his Bible and laid it beside his sleeping bag. He could see cars coming and going on his parents' driveway. The police and the press obviously were looking for a story. He slept all of Thursday night.

Jim woke up only once to the sound of thunder and a bolt of lightning that struck a tree nearby. The first traces of the rising sun were just appearing when he looked out of the cave.

The storm had passed, and the air and the earth seemed refreshed by its rain. He drank some water from the gallon jug beside him and ate some dried fruit. Then he turned to his Bible and the well-worn pages of First Kings. He found the passage that applied to him.

In it a mighty windstorm had struck the mountain, but the Lord was not in it. After the wind, there had been an earthquake, but the Lord was not in it. Then fire, but the Lord was not in the fire. Finally there was a gentle breeze, and the Lord was in it.

As Jim sat on the top of the bluff overlooking the countryside, he felt the gentle, rain-cleansed air moving by him. He knew with certainty that it was July 3rd. The Voice would speak to him. Today, his birthday, evil would be destroyed.

He looked to the east and watched a vision form slowly. The red of the fire number at the entrance to his parents' driveway burst forth from the pinks of the morning sun. Then the number appeared among the fading clouds on the horizon that had contained the night's storm. Three...three...three. The numbers were replaced by three long cylinders of red that had tips of gold.

"What do you see?" the Voice asked.

"I...I..." Jim stammered.

"What do you see?" The Voice grew more demanding.

The calm that Jim had experienced just moments before was quickly replaced by an excitement that had become all too familiar. He looked into the reds and golds of the sunrise and knew what he must do.

Rolling up his sleeping bag, Jim climbed down the side of the hill and walked to his car. The Voice was taking control of his mind, making it impossible to feel the bounce and sway of the car beneath him as he drove the wooded trail.

Without stopping, Jim turned on Grotzke Road and raced to his parents' driveway. The car fishtailed as he entered the drive. Only the dampness of the evening's rain kept the dust from churning up behind him. When he got to the house, he opened the car door and left it open as he raced up the steps. He did not see his mother in the kitchen. She must still be sleeping. His father, who had probably slept overnight in his rocking chair, yelled out in fright. Jim did not respond. Instead he went straight upstairs to his bedroom. He tore the curtain from the gun cabinet and threw it in a corner behind the bed.

Then he sat on his bed and studied the gun cabinet. The three red cylinders of destiny glowed as they stood on their brass ends. He touched one and quickly drew his hand back. Like the shells, his hand now glowed. The power within transferred itself into his very being.

The room seemed electric – its energies too much to be contained.

"Kill," the Voice demanded.

Jim took the three shells that had stood by the stocks of the guns.

"Kill!" the shrill Voice screamed throughout his mind.

Jim pulled his dad's Browning automatic from its resting place and pushed two of the slugs into the magazine. He drew the bolt back and let the first shell slide into the chamber. Then he pushed the third shell into the magazine and ran back down the stairs into the kitchen. His mother was still in bed. His dad looked at him and began to shout.

"The cops and reporters have been swarming all over this place looking for you. They said you ran a boat over the Wisconsin Dells dam and killed 125 people. You stupid asshole!"

The room was filled with the voices of devils taunting Jim. He was being tested, but this time the devil would not succeed.

"Where are you going with my shotgun? You can't take that!"

Jim hesitated. In the back of his mind he could feel the authority of his father's voice.

"Give me that gun! Look at you, you quivering little freak!" Mockery and scorn filled Ed's voice. "I may be confined to this chair, but I am still in control of you. I always have been since you were a child, and I always will be. Your own shame gives me control. Just stand there and think about it. You were so proud of that Bible your mother gave you, but I showed you the true meaning of all that rubbish.

"You were so proud, asking what this passage meant

and what that passage meant." Ed waved an arm, knocking his coffee can across the kitchen. It clattered off the wall and came to rest on the floor.

Jim put the shotgun on the kitchen table and tried to block the sound of his father's voice by putting his hands over his ears.

Ed shouted all the louder, trying to humiliate his son. "You came to me with that passage from the Book of Kings, and I showed you what it meant! Elijah took the widow's son and carried him upstairs and laid him on his bed. And then he stretched out on him three times and revived him. I showed you the meaning of that passage. Laid you on the bed and stretched out on you. Oh, did you come to life! Then I gave you back to your mother revived. You came to life every time I wanted you to after that. I control you! I am Elijah!"

Jim twisted his head between his hands struggling not to listen, but his father's voice kept breaking through. "I am Elijah! I am Elijah!" The pain and humiliation brought Jim to tears.

Ed was waving his arm and pointing a craggy finger at Jim. Spit flew from Ed's mouth as he continued to shout, "I am Elijah!"

Confusion overwhelmed Jim. Then the calm of the morning's gentle breeze blew through his mind. The Voice spoke. His confusion ended. He could not let the devil trick him. He had to take control. Jim took the shotgun from the table and pointed it at his father's midsection. "No. I am the new Elijah, and I am sending you to hell."

The deafening blast from the shotgun rocked the house and the double-hung window opposite Ed rattled in its casing. The impact of the slug almost tore Ed in half as it thrust him and the rocking chair against the wall. He bounced back and fell face forward on the floor. A trickle of blood turned into a flood under his body. The first devil shriveled before Jim's eyes and disappeared in a vapor.

The sound of the shot still echoed in Jim's ears as he

ran from the house and turned the old red and white Chevrolet toward Wisconsin Dells.

19

This was the first Friday of July, and Fr. Ross stood at the entrance of St. Bridget's talking to the larger than normal crowd that had attended the daily morning Mass. A custom dating back to the Middle Ages taught that if one made nine first-Friday Masses in a row, one was forgiven of all the punishment due for sins committed in this life. Many people in the post-Vatican Council era thought it was too mechanistic. Nevertheless, traditionalists still observed it. At St. Bridget's, confessions were scheduled right after the first Friday Mass. Most of the people had left, but a few were returning to church to receive the sacrament. Duke had gone down into the basement of the church to begin his chores, followed on this occasion by Rose Wells.

Police Chief Iverson pulled up in his squad car on the opposite side of the street just as Fr. Ross was dismissing the last of his parishioners. A squad car from neighboring Adams County pulled behind Iverson's car and parked. Iverson waved at Fr. Ross as both officers got out of their cars and started across the street.

"Krista Elliot called in a 911. Jim has gone berserk. She heard Jim and Ed shouting from her bedroom, but was afraid to come out. Then there was a gun shot, and Jim's car started up and roared down the driveway. When she went in the kitchen, Ed was lying in the middle of the floor dead. Krista saw the car turn at the end of the driveway in the direction of the Dells.

"Besides officers from Columbia County, I've called in units from Adams and Sauk counties. We just found Jim's car in the parking lot on the other side of the railroad tracks. I'm worried he may be after you again."

"Oh, no!" Iverson could feel the dismay in Fr. Ross' voice.

"Did you make sure all the doors in the rectory were locked when you came over for Mass?" Dan could tell by looking at Fr. Ross' face that he hadn't. In fact, he often left the side door open so Duke could walk over and wait for him to get back from Mass. They would have a cup of coffee together while discussing what work Duke was to do that day. Iverson knew, because he routinely stopped and waited for Fr. Ross to finish Mass and come back to the rectory. Any number of people followed the same procedure, and Fr. Ross always welcomed them to sit down and have coffee.

"I left the side door open."

"Damn it!" Iverson looked at the rectory as he formed a plan. "While you're finishing up, we're going to search the house. I don't want him in there waiting for you." The two officers turned and started walking down the sidewalk past the shrine to the Blessed Mother. Fr. Ross went back into the vestibule of the church. Voices were coming from the church basement. He listened closer and heard Rose asking Duke why he, Fr. Ross, had not returned her phone calls or been willing to let her make an appointment with him. He would have to ask Duke about the conversation during coffee.

As Fr. Ross pushed through the set of swinging doors that separated the vestibule from the main body of the church, he looked and made mental note of the fact that there were about six people kneeling toward the front of the church waiting to go to confession. He should be done just about the time Dan was through with his search of the rectory. They could have coffee together and he could ask Dan what was going on – if he should leave the Dells for the day for his own safety. But right now he was to hear confessions.

Turning, he approached the oak confessional boxes, still torn with the thought of not knowing whether he could have forgiven Jim for taking his life. Time had run out before he had been able to act as he lay on that altar. He had no answer. Our Lord had forgiven His persecutors. God had also entrusted him, through this sacrament, with the power of forgiveness. "Whose sins you shall forgive, they are forgiven. Whose sins you shall hold bound, they will be held bound." It was an awesome power. What if the one possessing that power could not carry it out in his own life?

Fr. Ross placed his hand on the familiar center door of the confessional. When he pulled it open, he knew the answer to the question. Standing in the place where the forgiveness of God normally flowed was unforgiving hate. Jim Elliot stood upright before him, a twelve-gauge shotgun held across his chest. Fr. Ross noticed only Jim's eyes. They were on fire. In that instant, Fr. Ross knew the answer. Sanity and holiness were gifts worth dying for. Forgive the person who had not found them.

Not a word was spoken. Fr. Ross moved back until he was against the back pew in the church and could move no more. Jim stepped out of the confessional, the gun pointing at Fr. Ross. The window of Elijah was directly behind the priest. The full force of the morning sun bathed the interior of the church in a red glow. For Jim, it spoke in a way it had never done before.

The blast of the shotgun threw Fr. Ross over the back of the pew and into the space between it and the next pew. He dropped on the seat and then slid to the floor. The second devil had disappeared.

Carrying the gun with him, Jim slammed through the swinging doors and into the vestibule. He would make his escape into the basement, through the tunnel under the street that connected the church and school, and out into the parking lot behind the school. He ran down the steps, but stopped upon entering the basement. Duke and Rose Wells were standing right in front of him. Duke, the very devil who had tricked him at the cemetery.

This was the reason for the third shell. Now all the devils would be gone from his life! The power of the new Elijah was about to triumph. The Voice urged him on. "Kill!"

Duke shoved Rose and tried to duck but the muzzle of the gun followed him. When the gun went off, Duke was lifted onto one of the tables set up for funeral dinners. He slid the length of it and fell to the floor out of Jim's sight. Rose remained, lying on the floor, screaming hysterically. Jim turned and pointed the shotgun at her. The firing pin clicked on an empty chamber. Rose would never hear it because of her own screams and the deafness caused by the muzzle blast in such a confined area.

Jim pulled open the heavy fire door in front of the tunnel, turned the light on and ran into its depths. At the opposite end he crossed the hallway and ran through the dining area. He threw the gun over the counter into the kitchen, pausing momentarily by the glass door leading into the parking lot. He didn't see anything that was a threat. He was only a block away from the railroad tracks, the parking lot, and the safety of his car.

At the sound of shots, Dan Iverson ran from the rectory to the church. The moment he entered the church he was on the radio. "Send an ambulance to St. Bridget's. We've had a shooting. If you are by that car in the parking lot, stay there! The suspect has got to be headed in that direction."

Leaving the other officer at the scene, Iverson ran out to his squad car, started the engine and turned off Oak Street onto LaCrosse. He knew Jim was somewhere between the school and the parking lot.

Jim could see Iverson coming up behind him as he crossed the railroad tracks. He ducked behind the embankment and looked back. Iverson had stopped. Jim knew he had to run for his car. As he entered the trees between the tracks and the parking lot, he saw the squad car beside his. He turned and ran north along the railroad tracks, using the trees to shield him from view. When he reached the parking lot entrance, he wanted to run under the railroad bridge and hide among the buildings along the street, but he couldn't. Iverson had to be coming down LaCrosse Street. They would meet right at the intersection. Even if Iverson wasn't coming, he could see him from where he was parked. The only escape route was the bridge across the Wisconsin River. Jim ran.

When he reached the other side of the bridge, he looked down the street toward the intersection at the bottom of the hill. Squad cars had stopped in the parking lot in front of Country Kitchen. The officers were out of their cars and looking up the hill toward the bridge, Iverson or the officers near his car must have seen him and alerted them.

Jim looked around. The power of Elijah calmed him. To his right was a chain link fence that surrounded Pirate's Cove, a miniature golf course carved into the side of a hill. A road that circled around to the top of the hill lay on the east side of it. Choosing the safety of all the shrubs and attractions inside, Jim jumped the fence and began the climb up the hill. It was still too early for most customers, and he avoided those he did see. He was just another tourist wandering around.

From the top of the hill, Jim could see the highway and the parking lots below. Squad cars were converging at the base of the hill from all directions. Somehow he had to fashion an escape. Jim turned, and the Voice spoke to him, "Elijah was carried by a whirlwind into the heavens." Jim looked, and there was the whirlwind sitting two flights of stairs above him – the helicopter used to take tourists on rides over the city.

They had tried to fry his brain before he left the Army. They had tried to burn all knowledge from his mind before they discharged him. He had told them he was Elijah and that he could lift himself up and disappear in a whirlwind and they had laughed. As a reward they had tried to fry his brain and alter it with drugs, but he had kept himself pure for this moment. From his hilltop in the country he had watched them flying overhead from the military base at Camp McCoy in Adams County. He had watched and practiced the art of flying one in his mind many times. He hadn't actually flown in years, but the lessons he had learned at Fort Rucker in Alabama were still fresh in his mind.

Now the Voice spoke in a way that took away all fear. He pushed aside the few customers waiting at the base of the hill. The sign on the gate read: "Crew and passengers only beyond this point." Jim shoved the gate open, pinning the attendant between it and the railing along the side of the steps. He cleared the steps and ran to the helicopter. The pilot was idling the rotors between loads of tourists. Jim grabbed the buckle on the front of the pilot's seat belt and released it. Then he pulled the pilot through the door and sent him tumbling to the base of the lift-off pad.

The Hughes 500 D was a two-seat helicopter that held four passengers and a pilot. Jim looked out through the bubble front. Police officers were coming up the hill from all directions. He sat there for a moment, the rotors idling above and behind him. The whirlwind of Elijah surrounded him.

Jim placed his feet on the pedals that controlled the pitch of the tail rotor. Next he reached for the collective stick and the throttle on the left side of his seat. This would change the pitch of the blades above and lift him into the air. Then he grabbed the Cyclyic stick with his right hand. Once he was in the air the Cyclyic stick gave him the ability to move forward or backward, right or left. Glancing at the TOT, oil pressure and other gauges, Jim began to rev the jet engine. He could feel the increase of wind through the open door beside him. The helicopter lifted from the pad and then hesitated. The winds were from the south, and Jim knew he had to head into them, but first he paused to relish the moment. He had wanted this job at the Dells, had applied for it year after year, but they had always turned him down. Now he would show them. While tourists and staff were picking themselves off the grass, Jim looked down on them from his place of command. He watched the police officers scrambling below and thought if only it was a military helicopter he would show them a real chariot of fire.

Looking over his left shoulder, Jim recognized the squad car parked in the lot in front of the ticket booth for the helicopter ride. It was Iverson. He was out of his patrol car and walking around behind it. Laughter filled the cockpit of the helicopter. That was the beautiful thing about it. Even if they could reach up and snatch him from the sky and kill him, it didn't matter. He would go to heaven. But they weren't going to kill him. He was out of pistol range.

Dan Iverson knew he didn't have much time. He opened the trunk of the car and reached inside for his Winchester Model 70 seven-millimeter magnum. Unzipping the end of the case, he pulled the gun out and placed two shells in the magazine and a third in the chamber. Using the top of his car as a rest Dan steadied the scope on the helicopter above. He saw Jim through the opening in the side. The helicopter turned and began to head south. Dan was left with the rear and the bottom of the helicopter as his target. The two fuel cells on the Hughes 500 D rested side by side under the floor. Iverson fired three times.

The helicopter turned slightly. Smoke poured from one of the bullet holes, followed by flame. The helicopter began its descent on the opposite side of the highway over the Wisconsin River and its dam. It was still in the air when it exploded, showering pieces over the rock cliff that formed the riverbank between the Lighthouse Restaurant and the dam.

20

Krista sat on the porch of the farmhouse. She had packed her few belongings in a cardboard box and put them beside her chair. Bernice Evans was coming to take her to the nursing home. She ran her hand between the buttons on the front of her dress. She could feel the hard scar of a cigarette burn on the bottom of her breast. The county had buried her husband and her son. She hadn't attended either burial. She couldn't forgive her husband. She couldn't find the words to apologize to her son for bringing him into the world.

Dan Iverson had visited her. The police had pried open the trunk of Jim's car, where they found a number of things. Some explained his long absence, particularly his medical discharge from the Army, something he had never told her about. There were hospital forms, prescriptions, and books checked out of libraries that gave hints of where he had traveled. He still had his military manuals of instructions for helicopter flight.

Dates on unused prescriptions and in the back of the library books put him in the vicinity of a number of priest murders. Until now they had seemed isolated incidents. It was obvious that Fr. Ross was not the first priest who, Jim felt, lacked the power to cleanse him.

Krista gazed out at her garden. Without her care the weeds would soon take over. In her world evil had often overpowered the good. She looked down at the crucifix she had taken from the wall and placed on top of her clothes. She begged God to reaffirm her faith in the fact that good always triumphs in the end.

Duke drifted in and out of consciousness as he lay in his hospital bed in the Baraboo Hospital. The dream was always the same. He had died and was in a long passageway filled with brilliant light. He was at peace. He moved in concert with a long procession of others dressed in white robes. As he approached a boundary that separated him from a set of golden buildings, a figure approached him. He looked beneath the hood and saw his father's face. His blue eyes sparkled. The deep pores were still in his tanned cheeks.

His father smiled and said, "You have to go back."

Duke pressed forward only to be met by his dad's parents. "You have to go back," they insisted.

It was hard for Duke to do so. He enjoyed the peace of this new world, felt attracted to the golden city. Besides, he felt he had completed his mission. Hadn't he saved Fr. Ross in the cemetery and Rose in the church basement?

"You have to go back." Duke's dad had now joined the grandparents.

Reluctantly he turned and began the return trip through the passageway. On the opposite side of an invisible barrier he saw a stream of white hooded people on their way toward eternity. They were faceless except for one figure. It was Fr. Ross. He moved by Duke without a sign of recognition. The barrier prevented Duke's speaking to him. Duke wondered if Fr. Ross would be turned back, too.

Duke twisted his head on the pillow. His eyelids opened slowly to see Dan Iverson sitting beside his bed.

"You were lucky," Duke heard Iverson saying as if Iverson felt he had been conscious for a long time. "The shotgun slug caught you in the side when you jumped to push Rose. It tore a couple ribs up pretty bad, but you are going to live."

"What about Fr. Ross?"

Before Iverson could reply, Rose Wells burst into the room. She was wearing tight jean shorts and a blouse with a neckline that started to dip at her shoulders. Her hair was now dyed red to match her present choice of apparel. Her high heels clicked on the terrazzo floor as she ran toward the hospital bed.

"You saved my life! You are my hero. I must have been blind all this time not to see my fourth husband right in my very midst. I love you!"

"I'll come back," Iverson said as he made his way to the door.

Rose grabbed Duke's head with both hands. Then she leaned forward and stuffed his face between her breasts.

Duke fumbled for the nurse's call button. Why must he return?